Young Writers 2005 Creative Writing Competition For Secondary Schools

From Southern England
Edited by Lynsey Hawkins

Disclaimer

Young Writers has maintained every effort
to publish stories that will not cause offence.

Any stories, events or activities relating to individuals
should be read as fictional pieces and not construed
as real-life character portrayal.

First published in Great Britain in 2005 by:
Young Writers
Remus House
Coltsfoot Drive
Peterborough
PE2 9JX
Telephone: 01733 890066
Website: www.youngwriters.co.uk

All Rights Reserved

© Copyright Contributors 2005

SB ISBN 1 84602 222 3

Foreword

Young Writers was established in 1991 and has been passionately devoted to the promotion of reading and writing in children and young adults ever since. The quest continues today. *Young Writers* remains as committed to engendering the fostering of burgeoning poetic and literary talent as ever.

This year, *Young Writers* are happy to present a dynamic and entertaining new selection of the best creative writing from a talented and diverse cross section of some of the most accomplished secondary school writers around. Entrants were presented with four inspirational and challenging themes.

'Myths And Legends' gave pupils the opportunity to adapt long-established tales from mythology (whether Greek, Roman, Arthurian or more conventional eg The Loch Ness Monster) to their own style.

'A Day In The Life Of …' offered pupils the chance to depict twenty-four hours in the lives of literally anyone they could imagine. A hugely imaginative wealth of entries were received encompassing days in the lives of everyone from the top media celebrities to historical figures like Henry VIII or a typical soldier from the First World War.

Finally 'Short Stories', in contrast, offered no limit other than the author's own imagination while 'Hold The Front Page' provided the ideal opportunity to challenge the entrants' journalistic skills, asking them to provide a newspaper or magazine article on any subject of their choice.

T.A.L.E.S. From Southern England is ultimately a collection we feel sure you will love, featuring as it does the work of the best young authors writing today.

Contents

Archbishop Tenison's CE School, Croydon
Emma Morton (14)	1
Carine Packer (14)	2
Greg Lee (14)	3
James Smith	4
Stephanie Wood (14)	6
Stéphane Rouschmeyer (14)	7
David Marley (14)	8
Hakeem Adelakun (14)	9
Adele Warne (14)	10
Maria Wake (14)	11

Bishopsgate School, Egham
Rebecca Dobson (12)	12
Kareem Raslan (12)	13
Jonathan Kahn (11)	14
Michael White (11)	15
Alice Jamison (10)	16
Matthew Main (11)	17
Benjamin Brebner (11)	18
Jessica Cartwright (11)	19
Alberto Leoni-Sceti (11)	20
Amy Osborne (11)	21
Michael Lombardo (10)	22
Benjamin Clarke (11)	23
Jamie Sayer (11)	24
Tom Rich (12)	25
James Simcox (12)	26
Luke Daines (12)	28
William Locke (12)	29
George Irons (12)	30
Jack Lowe (12)	32

George Abbot School, Guildford
Rhiannon Pratt (11)	34
Elizabeth Hogg (12)	35
Megan Barber (12)	36
Rebekah Smith (12)	37

Fergus Bell (12)	38
Hannah Blackwood (14)	39
Ritchie Lord (12)	40
William James (12)	41
Sam Jewell (11)	42
Lloyd Stephens (11)	43
Katie Butchers (12)	44
Amy Danilewicz (12)	45

Haling Manor High School, South Croydon
Rachel Price (13)	46

Horndean Technology College, Waterlooville
Lilly Emeney (13)	48
Samantha Leimanis (12)	49
Lorna Salmon (14)	50
Kayleigh Robins (14)	51
Hannah Watson (12)	52
Lisa-Jayne Wiseman (14)	53
Kirsty Claridge (14)	54

Limington House School, Basingstoke
Simon Thomas (15)	55

Mayville High School, Southsea
Jordan Knight (12)	56
Zahra Jaffer (11)	57
Elisabeth Welfare (12)	58
Sayyeda-Maryam Gangji (12)	59
Victoria O'Brien (12)	60
Georgina Cullen (11)	61
Eliza Castleton (12)	62
Soraya Al-Mahrouq (13)	63
James MacFarlane (13)	64
Jacques Voller (12)	65
Tom Petty (11)	66
Sophie Tomkins (12)	67
Rhys Owen (12)	68

Milton Abbey School, Blandford Forum

Matthew Williams (15)	69
Nick Turner (17)	70
Alexander Shepherd (16)	71
Thomas Poate (15)	72
James Whitlock (15)	73
Samuel Gell (18)	74
Tom Barrow (15)	75
George Le Gallais (15)	76
Nicolas Rainey (15)	77
Richard Hagenbuch (15)	78
Hugo Mann (15)	79
Michael Gell (15)	80

Moyles Court School, Ringwood

Nathan Barry (14)	81
Danny Whitelock (12)	82
Oliver Hayter (12)	83
Dalton North (13)	84
Samantha Buck (12)	85
Shaunie Huzzey (12)	86
Sarah Dickinson (13)	87
Bethany Hume (12)	88
Cameron Leverell Oag (13)	89
Alexander Haigh (12)	90
Matthew Haynes (14)	91
Oliver Unt (14)	92
Gemma Fraser (13)	93
Mali Griffiths (13)	94
Ryan Saunders (13)	95
Edward Hodgson-Egan (13)	96
Kirsty Osborne (14)	97
George Soan (13)	98

Philip Southcote School, Addlestone

Adam Leslie (14)	99
John Hockley (14)	100

Staunton Park Community School, Havant
Sophie Jackson (13)   101
Michaela George (12)   102

Swanmore Middle School, Ryde
Rebecca Jones (13)   103
Nicolle Hodges (12)   104
Jade Smith (13)   105
Max Sampson (13)   106
Jessica Pegram (12)   107
Joe Peduzzi (11)   108
Ellie Brentnall (12)   109
Rachel Sheath (12)   110
Kate Nutbourne (12)   112
Stacey Downer (12)   113
Letitia Mitchell (12)   114
Phil Hodges (12)   115
Elliot Winsor-Viney (12)   116
James Dighton (12)   117
Becky Saxcoburg (13)   118
Scott Wraxton (12)   119
Megan Wingate (13)   120
Poppy Yeo (13)   121
Amii Stansfield (13)   122
Robert Clark (13)   123
Shelley Rickard-Worth (13)   124
Sadie Tompkins-McLean (12)   125
Carl Everett (12)   126

Sycamore Centre, Epsom
Daniel Sleet (13)   127
James Stiff (16)   128
Jack Gibson (13)   130
Brett Carslake (15)   131

The Blandford School, Blandford Forum
Patrick Coker   132
Nathan Kirby (14)   133
Ryan Keogh (14)   134
Mike Wyatt (13)   135

Kieran Davidson	136
Henry Baggridge (14)	137
Tim Bevington-King (14)	138
Richard Hoyt (13)	139
Dario Roncaglia (14)	140
Courtney Samways	141
Craig Sutherland (14)	142
Justin Hall (14)	143
Neil Chivers (14)	144
Katie Shorto (14)	145
Hannah Garrett (13)	146
Zoe Greenfield (14)	147
Harriet Cunningham (13)	148
Marie Christine Cowgill (13)	149
Harry Eves (14)	150
Jess Ryall (14)	151
Christian Swann (13)	152
Emma Damon	153
Tom Cox (14)	154
Laura Dewhurst (14)	155
April Orchard (14)	156
Jaz Arwand	157
Rory Loxton	158
Verity Ockenden (13)	159
Elliot Edwards (13)	160
Nathan Jeffries (14)	161
Matt Veal (13)	162
Tom New (14)	163
Kieran Tickner-Hinkes (13)	164
Daniel Daly (14)	165
Jamie Chadd (14)	166
Helen Miller (14)	167
Zoë Lamb (13)	168
Catherine Abraham	169
Hannah Bissett (14)	170
Hannah Manson (14)	171
Jodie Cooper (14)	172
Chris Taafe	173
Alex Robbins (14)	174
Alexander Lyes (14)	175
Raph Lee (14)	176
Perrie Staley-Crouch (13)	177

Yvette Lowe (15)	178
Carly Morris (13)	179
Shauni Paulley (15)	180
Kieran Harvey (15)	181
Michelle Kisbee (14)	182
Kelly Wareham (14)	183
Emma Taylor (14)	184
Holly McGowan Hayes (14)	185
Aimee Dunbar	186
Jason Craig (14)	187

Treloar School, Alton

Therese Hunt (15)	188
Jamie Woods (15)	189
Matthew Gunning (15)	190
Jonathan Grant-Said (16)	191
Fay Hart (15)	192
Jessica Parrott (13)	193

Wildern School, Southampton

Aidan Rennie-Jones (12)	194
Christie Grattan (13)	195
Jonathan Knapp (12)	196

Woodroffe School, Lyme Regis

Jessica Shute (12)	197
Daniel Stokes (12)	198
Megan Ruddick (12)	199
Pollyanna Mowbray (12)	200
Noah Hillyard (13)	201
Laura Davenport (14)	202
Poppie Stevens (14)	203
Jennifer Watts (12)	204
Suzie Riley (14)	205
Maisie Conlon (14)	206
Jack Borthwick (13)	207
Jack Lamb-Wilson (13)	208
Ben Elliott (14)	209
Bethany Chick (12)	210
Emma Bowditch (12)	211

Jonathan Moore (12)	212
Camilla Johnstone (14)	213
Ellen Faithfull (12)	214
Amanda Cowling (12)	216

The Creative Writing

What Happened To Time?

As I ran home I sensed something was not quite right. I approached the door and put the key in the lock but it didn't turn, it would not open. I slammed my hand on the bell and waited.

No one came. I frantically pressed the bell three more times but there was no reply. What was I to do? We'd only moved in two days ago, it was a strange neighbourhood and I knew no one. I was frustrated and pushed the door with all my force; it opened and as I walked through I gasped. The walls had changed colour and all the moving boxes had gone. What had happened? Where was I?

I cautiously opened the living room door and stepped inside. I stood, rooted to the spot, horrified at the sight in front of me. A man in a black cloak was towering over a quivering woman on the floor. Blood was seeping through her chest and there was a dagger in the man's hand.

The man threw his cloak over himself and disappeared. I was astonished and scared but remembering the woman, ran towards her. I knelt down, panic, fear and anxiety flooded me … it was my mother.

'Who are you?' she whimpered, her last words. I was astounded as I let go of her hand. I suddenly noticed how yes she was my mum but a lot younger. Much younger. I cried with confusion and pain as she died. Where on earth was I and what had happened?

Emma Morton (14)
Archbishop Tenison's CE School, Croydon

A Day In The Life Of ...

The one, the only Angel Smith ... confused? Yes ... that's because it's me ... my real name is Angela but Angel for when I'm famous.

So tonight ladies and gentlemen Angela is going to be ... Angela Smith. No, not impressed? Well trust me my life is fab! Imagine a mansion, a million pounds in the money box and everything that is *wow!* Still not impressed? Well maybe the truth will be a start eh?

I live in a small four bedroom house with a swimming pool. OK I'll stop! A four bedroom house, with two very annoying sisters who simply just love clothes and money. I wouldn't waste my money on clothes. Exploring is more my thing and animal research and examining ... swiftly moving on.

Well ... I go to a public school and get in a fight nearly every day, as the boys just won't leave me alone. They call me 'the black sheep' as I'm the odd one out.

My life's pretty simple, wake up, school, go home, wake up, school, go home. Why be J-Lo doing practically anything you want, when you can be Angela Smith? I wouldn't change me for anyone. When I'm famous and people want a ride in my jet, I will be kind and say, 'Bye,' from the window! My life is simple but sometimes simple is better.

Carine Packer (14)
Archbishop Tenison's CE School, Croydon

A Day In The Life Of A Dog

My life isn't all it's cracked up to be. All I seem to do nowadays is eat, sleep and go for the occasional walk down at the park. I don't mind doing these things but I feel that I'm missing out in life. Here is my daily routine:

At about seven in the morning I am woken up by my owner and at half-past eight in the morning I eat my breakfast ... which is Pedigree dog biscuits mixed in with a chicken-flavoured jelly ... nice. I wish I could enjoy other food, which is why, whenever my owner is eating and something falls to the floor, it's mine for the taking.

After breakfast I enjoy a nice long nap in the sun. I normally get rudely awakened by my owner coming down the stairs quite loudly, but I shrug it off and go back to sleep.

At about half-past three in the afternoon and a quarter past nine at night, my owner takes me on my walks to the park. I usually see my doggy friends there, such as Ed the cocker spaniel, Cynthia the poodle and Lord the bulldog. My owner doesn't let me play with them at night-time but I can during the day.

I get home after my walk and head for my bed and instantly fall asleep. What a day. I guess I'm used to this lifestyle, hey, it's a dog's life.

Greg Lee (14)
Archbishop Tenison's CE School, Croydon

The Talking Hamburger

Hello, my name's Davey the hamburger! My best friends are called Chips and Coca-Cola. Chips is very skinny and Coca-Cola isn't fat or skinny, but I'm very fat. I go everywhere with them and this is the story of our adventure.

Ding-dong!
'Oh hello Mrs Wedgey is Chips home?'
'Yes Davey he is, I'll go get him for you.'
'Oh hello Chips, I'm so excited about our camping trip.'
'Yeah me too, now let's go get Coca-Cola.'
Knock, knock!
'You OK Coca-Cola?'
'Yeah, I'm fine thanks.'

Now this is the bit that Chips and me weren't ready to hear. It started with Chips saying, 'You don't look OK to me Coca-Cola, you look sad.'
'Well I've got something to tell you two.'
'What is it?'
'Well, I heard that where we are going to camp, it's haunted!'
'What, are you sure? How do you know?'
'Well it came on the news that other foods were disappearing!'
Then I said bravely, 'Who cares? Now come on you two.'

'Right, we're here and oh look, no ghosts, dead bodies or anything.'
'I've got a bad feeling you guys.'
'Fine then you two scaredy weeds, stay here, I'll get the wood.'

Now I'd advise you to stop reading here because this is the scary bit and here's a secret, I'm talking to you from food heaven so you know it's scary from here on!

'Hmm!'
'What was that?'
'Probably nothing.'
'Mummy, I want that big, fat, juicy burger there!'
'Ha! Help!'

I was running and running. I felt something on my bun and started screaming.

'Ahhh!'

Crunch.

I died.

James Smith
Archbishop Tenison's CE School, Croydon

A Day In The Life Of Sophia

My name is Sophia. I am fifteen years old and I live in a hut with my younger sister Rahima and my mother.

Since my father died seven years ago, we have lost all our money and we also lost our home, which is why we live in a tiny hut.

My mother cannot work because she cannot read or write, so nobody will employ her. My sister Rahima (who is ten) and I, used to try and teach Mother to read, but we cannot do that anymore because we no longer attend school as Mother cannot afford the fees. Because of this Rahima and I are not able to read or write well.

During the day I work on a nearby farm for nine hours and I earn six pounds each day. I do not enjoy this job at all because I often get mocked by rich people in nice clothes because I am poor, but I have to maintain this job because I have to do it for Mother, otherwise we would have no money at all.

Rahima is too young to work but she fetches water from the lake for bathing and drinking as the hut has no electricity or water supply.

Strictly we are not even meant to be living there, but we have no choice. Each day I live in fear of being homeless and I feel like I am responsible for this family now that it has been torn apart. Everything has been ruined.

Stephanie Wood (14)
Archbishop Tenison's CE School, Croydon

A Day In The Life Of A Hair

Darkness comes and we feel free again. Many strands of hair have fallen, been ripped and one burnt today. I should tell this story from the start.

In the morning as we wake, we are all mixed together, but no one noticed until after the shower. In the shower we are pulled, ripped and damaged as the shampoo is applied and burns us right to our roots. At least 12 hair strands die and fall out at this moment.

After the shower, we are left alone for about 10 minutes. Then comes the comb. We call it *the Comb of Death!* You can understand why this is, seeing as we are ripped out in large groups and many dead hairs are left on the teeth of the comb. We lose around 20 men here.

During the day, we are tied, untied, pulled, combed, straightened, struck in small bands and places ... this makes us lose the most amount of strands in a day. We lose on average 50 strands during a day. Some long, some short and some like me, still growing.

Some nights, like earlier, we are faced with the special treatment - change of colour, shortening, cleaning, styling etc. It can be great fun if it doesn't go wrong for you!

My owner decided that I was too grey so I was now lying on my own in the bin. What will happen this time when darkness comes?

Stéphane Rouschmeyer (14)
Archbishop Tenison's CE School, Croydon

A Day In The Life Of Mr Main

Mr Main is my teacher. He teaches Year 6 at Weighbridge Primary School.

Last Monday, he came in expecting a perfectly normal day. Most of the morning was okay, except for when Bobby Stone threw chewing gum in Sarah May's hair, but otherwise it was fine.

After he spent break standing outside with his hot mug of coffee, he went back to his class where he could hear laughing. As he entered the class he saw his mother teaching the class science and telling them about the time he wet himself on his first day of school!

After he made his mother leave it was lunch so he stumbled into the staffroom and buried himself under some paperwork.

When he went back to his classroom, he found a note from the head teacher saying he'd taken the children to the box factory. He sat in his chair, put his feet up and fell asleep.

After a pleasant dream about Smarties and Rolos, his trusty mother woke him up and took him back to her house.

When he arrived, his dad wished his mum happy birthday. After saying he'd do anything to make her feel better, she told him to sing some songs he used to sing in the choir!

Now that I, a pupil, found this story in his diary, on his desk, I will never fail a test again!

David Marley (14)
Archbishop Tenison's CE School, Croydon

A Day In The Life Of Patrick Vieira

Every morning is the same as the last. I get up the same time as always, I have a shower and brush my teeth. Sometimes I have breakfast and sometimes I don't depending on how I feel and then I sit down and watch the TV.

Today I have training so I get dressed, grab my boots and head off. On the way I drop by and pick up Henry and Pires, who is nearly always late, to come down for the ride and it was the same again today but in the end we always seem to get there on time!

When we get there, Wenger is already there which is no real surprise and he has everything set up. I go into the changing room and get changed into my boots, go outside and start kicking around the balls till Wenger is ready to call us over.

After training, I take a shower and then go upstairs to play pool as usual and I thrash Dennis at it.

Most of the time after training we all go home and then come back and meet at one of the player's houses and today we're going to Ashley's. Today we're hoping to play a prank on Dennis.

At Ashley's house we just talk and sometimes play 'Pro 4' then we go home.

When I get home I either just watch some TV or go straight to bed. Every day is quite the same and I get very used to it.

Hakeem Adelakun (14)
Archbishop Tenison's CE School, Croydon

Searching

After I told him to look after my memories I ran, took one look back at my burning village and ran. I had nowhere to go but to the wolves. It took me weeks to find them as they had been travelling for five years. Luckily for me they remembered me and took me in straight away. I became their leader.

After spending a year away from him I couldn't stand it. I missed him. Even if I did betray him he would still forgive me. Although life with the wolves was great I still felt like something was missing from my life.

I started my journey back to the old village but he wasn't there. All that remained there were the bones from where the battle had taken place.

Every night I sit and cry. Everywhere I go it reminds me of him. I have nightmares again but this time I know why. In my dreams he stands there, his white hair, his black hands bring out the knife and then he slaughters them again.

On my travels I found another village where the dark horse was attacked. A boy about a year older than me asked me to take him with me. His family were taken by them. As it was partly my fault I agreed. This didn't slow me down on my journey though.

A serpent told me he'd seen Sidguard. When I arrived at the place he told me there was a figure about Sidguard's height and looked like him from the back. Then he turned around …

Adele Warne (14)
Archbishop Tenison's CE School, Croydon

A Day In The Life Of A Book

I get rudely awoken at 7am and slung into a bag. There I lie for half an hour in the dark. Every so often I see the light of day, as more stuff joins me. At the end of it all I am squashed right at the bottom with sandwiches on top of me.

7.30am comes and I start to get thrown around in the bag; we must be on our way to the bus stop. It definitely feels colder. To add to it all, the immature exercise books are making a racket and all I want to do is have a nap.

The bus arrives (late as usual) and there is a seat. It looks like my services will be needed. I see a giant hand coming towards me and it navigates its way to me. I am opened, oh how much my back aches and every time a page is turned it sends shivers down my spine.

The bus journey finally ends and I can have a rest. I am not used for the rest of the day; other things come and go but I stay put, waiting till I'm needed again.

At 7pm my time comes and I am finally taken out of the bag and brought into the comfort of the bedroom. This time the turning of the pages is quite relaxing, it is like a comforting massage.

After about an hour I am gently placed on a bedside table, ready and waiting. Services to be used again.

Maria Wake (14)
Archbishop Tenison's CE School, Croydon

My Diary: Escape From Schnel

Day 1: Monday May 16th, 1943

I woke, only to feelings of confusion of where I was. I looked around me, saw many faces that I knew. It then came to me that they were in my squadron. I knew that something was wrong because everyone was silent. I asked the guy next to me where we were. He told me something I really already knew, he told me that we were on our way to the nearest POW camp. My face fell, even though this came as no surprise. I looked around me again and now I knew why everyone looked so gloomy.

We got out of the truck. It looked the same as every other camp that I'd seen and escaped from.

The Germans took us to our designated huts. Most of the men in my squad went to hut 3 as well as me and the rest to hut 5. As I went in everyone dashed past me to the nearest bed they wanted. We all went for a look around the camp for blind spots and easy escape routes.

That night we all talked of escape as many of us had been in POW camps too many times to remember. We discussed old escape plans that might work, but many of them were no use for this camp.

Rebecca Dobson (12)
Bishopsgate School, Egham

Escape From A POW Camp - Hearthen Harr

Escape Day

Escape time. I have called a meeting just before we escape. This meeting will include final instructions as well as me wishing the group the best of luck. Everyone was here and ready, we were about to go.

'Everyone, this may possibly be the last time we ever see each other again. If we don't see anyone in this room ever again, then just remember us in spirit. Your final instructions are this. Once we get out onto the farmland, you run, don't look back, just forward. As most of you can already tell, it is already dark. No one will see you as you are running. Here are the fake bills of money, all your IDs in case something happens to you and everyone, here are your uniforms.'

I stopped for a while, this was for them to put their uniforms on and get used to the things I had just given them. Then I started again. I realised I had to make this final speech a good one as this may be the last speech that I'd be giving …

'First of all we need to get those poor souls out of solitary confinement. Once that is done, the whole escape will be finished. After you leave this tunnel, it is not going to be a group effort anymore, but an individual effort. It's going to be tough surviving out there, but I feel you guys have what it takes. It has been a real pleasure leading you and I assure you that this group definitely have the passion.'

Kareem Raslan (12)
Bishopsgate School, Egham

Brawl Of The Day

A brawl has just happened resulting in the death of Mercutio, Tybalt and the banishment of Romeo. This is an eyewitness account from Benvolio. 'It was a horrible fight. Tybalt called Romeo a villain and Mercutio defending Romeo's pride fought Tybalt but paid the price of his life, then Romeo, avenging Mercutio's death, killed Tybalt'.

This was what ladies of both houses said, 'Romeo was only obeying the law when killing Tybalt as Mercutio had been killed by Tybalt, so the young man had done nothing wrong'.

The Prince of Verona who is currently mourning over the death of his kinsman had decided not to kill Romeo but banish him from Verona.

Jonathan Kahn (11)
Bishopsgate School, Egham

Day Of Mourning For The House Of Capulet And The House Of Montague

Yesterday, a tragic day for both the Montagues and the Capulets, as both Mercutio and Tybalt met their death. At the same time Romeo was banished from the city of fair Verona.

The whole of Verona is in mourning for these two bright youths, who died so nobly fighting for their honour and their houses.

A fight broke out in the early evening yesterday in the market square. Mercutio picked a fight with Tybalt and Romeo attempted to separate the two youths. Tybalt stabbed Mercutio in the neck and he fell to the ground to his early death.

Romeo sought revenge for Mercutio's death, attacked Tybalt with his sword and killed him instantly. A small number of friends from both houses watched in horror as their tragic drama unfolded before their eyes.

An eyewitness at the scene at the time said, 'Tybalt was leaning against a pillar when Mercutio, Romeo and me walked past him. He stuck his foot out and tripped up Mercutio. Tybalt had started the fight.

The three of us turned round and Tybalt insulted Romeo and challenged him to fight him, but Romeo ignored the challenge and moved away.

Mercutio wanted to defend the honour of his house and in doing so, sadly fell to his death.

Romeo ran after Tybalt who suddenly stopped and turned round to face Romeo.

They began to fight, Romeo stabbed Tybalt and Tybalt fell and like Mercutio, was taken by death'.

The prince was soon at the scene and demanded an explanation from those who had seen what had happened. Deciding that Romeo had not started the fight and was not his fault, banished him from the city.

A sad day indeed for both Capulets and Montagues.

Michael White (11)
Bishopsgate School, Egham

Dealing With Disastrous Death And Breathtaking Banishing!

Yesterday was a very tragic day when Tybalt Capulet and Mercutio had a fight till their death. It then ended when Romeo said, 'Stop it. Enough is enough'. Tybalt then lashed out and stabbed Mercutio. Romeo was not happy about this so he forced his sword through Tybalt's chest. Both men lay there in distress (especially Tybalt) while Romeo tried to comfort Mercutio.

Suddenly Benvolio found Tybalt and reported Romeo straight away.

Lady Capulet ordered a death sentence, but luckily for Romeo the law saved him. This was because Tybalt stabbed Mercutio first.

Juliet had been grieving at losing Tybalt, but also at losing the love of her life, Romeo.

There will be more detailed news tomorrow.

Alice Jamison (10)
Bishopsgate School, Egham

Romeo's Last Letter

Dear Lord Montague, Father,

By the time you read this letter I shall be dead. Lying next to my one true love, Juliet. I am so sorry that I kept this so secret, but I love Juliet. I have married a Capulet. I am sorry. Please forgive me, I beg of you.

I am going to take this poison I bought from an apothecary. Juliet is dead, I will die beside her. I do not regret buying that poison. I do not regret killing Tybalt, he deserved to die. Mercutio was killed by Tybalt. Mercutio was my best friend. I killed Tybalt, he was in my way, and I do not regret loving Juliet and marrying her.

I love you my lord,
Your son always,
Romeo.

Matthew Main (11)
Bishopsgate School, Egham

Romeo's Last Letter

Dearest Father and Mother,

I have not been who I seem. By the time this last letter of mine reaches you, I will be dead. I have a confession to make: My true love is that of sweet Juliet Capulet. The friar has married Juliet and I in eternal harmony, but now we are eternally divorced. I beg your kindest apology and forgiveness for the slaying of the noble Tybalt and the death of Mercutio, who was my dearest friend, under my restraining arm.

I have not been a good son for my name is not of Montague but of traitor, for I have many skeletons in my bedchamber. One of which is the vile potion of which I bought from the poorest apothecary in Mantua's dark alleyways, and its cold form will be my demise. I now lie with my dearest and only love, Juliet, in the Capulets' tomb, never to be disturbed by the living again while I sleep in eternal death.

Again I beg your forgiveness, for never will you again see me.

Your dearest son,

Romeo Montague.

Benjamin Brebner (11)
Bishopsgate School, Egham

Romeo's Last Letter

Dear Father,

I have disobeyed you Father. I have a confession to make: I am married to Juliet of our rivals the Capulets. I know she is our archenemy but I love her and need her like a flower to water. I beg for your forgiveness of my actions. As I have heard of her death I have brought some poison that I will take at Juliet's tomb tonight where I will kiss her dead, frozen lips for the very last time. I have shame and blood on my conscience because I slayed Tybalt.

Love from

Your dearest Romeo.

Jessica Cartwright (11)
Bishopsgate School, Egham

Bloody Beowulf Beats Up Grendel

Two days ago, at the magnificent great hall of Heorot, arrived the great warrior called Beowulf. Beowulf the well-known leader of the Goths, came to Heorot all the way from the other side of the world, over freezing ice caps and scorching sand dunes, on a quest to kill the evil monster, Grendel, who lives deep in the dark forest of Ugrael, in a deep, deep and dreary pool where no living creature has yet dared to set foot, until now.

But killing Grendel was not enough for the brave warrior. After killing Grendel he went after the bigger, meaner and deadlier, the one and only - Grendel's mother.

Beowulf set off with 15 of his fellow Goths but also with 5 of the great king's men. They trudged through the dark forest of Ugrael where unknown creatures of the deep lived. The brave men did not meet any such creatures on their journey but encountered the men of the forest. The men of the forest are mysterious creatures who have human features but the minds of beasts.

Beowulf managed to make a deal with the men, for the men had been having trouble with their food lately and blamed Grendel and his mom for it.

The deal consisted of Beowulf managing to get rid of Grendel and his mother, and the men of the Ugrael Forest would let them be, but also they would let them have one of their huts to sleep in for the night for it had grown dark in the already dark forest.

The forest men agreed to the deal and the men went to the hut and slept.

In the morning, when the forest men woke up, their was no sign of Beowulf or his men for they had awoken very early to continue their way through the dangerous forest.

At long last they arrived at the monster's lair, which was a small pond in which deep, deep down was Grendel's cave. But the cave had a sort of magic spell that kept the water, from the small pond, out of the underwater cave. Beowulf jumped into the pond without hesitating and straight away was grabbed by Grendel's mother and dragged down. They had a bloody and terrible fight but in the end Beowulf chopped her head off and swam up carrying the head with him.

Alberto Leoni-Sceti (11)
Bishopsgate School, Egham

Romeo's Last Letter

Dear Father,

I deeply regret all that you have done for me but now I must confess my sins and the love that I have for Juliet, but two days ago Juliet and I got married despite her sadness about Tybalt.

Now my dear wife is dead so I have nothing left in my life. I have bought a bottle of poison from a poor apothecary that will let me lie in peace with her for evermore.

I am sorry if I have disappointed you but I am just doing what I think is best for myself as I am a man now.

Your beloved son,
Romeo.

Amy Osborne (11)
Bishopsgate School, Egham

Romeo's Last Letter

Dear Father,
 By the time you read this I shall be dead! So I must confess that I have disobeyed you, I have married Juliet, a Capulet!
 Please, please, please forgive me, but do not stay angry at me, I did it out of love! I also have to say it is my fault for the death of Mercutio. I would not stand up for myself when Tybalt was calling me names so Mercutio got angry, fought Tybalt and then he was killed.
 You may be wondering why I am going to kill myself, it is because I cannot live without Juliet. So I bought some poison from a poor apothecary and now I shall lay next to her in the Capulet tomb in eternal death. I am sorry and I will miss you.
 Sincerely,
 Romeo.

Michael Lombardo (10)
Bishopsgate School, Egham

Romeo's Last Letter

Dear Father,

I am sorry to have kept this secret from you so long, regardless of the name and feud, I, against everybody's will, have married Juliet Capulet. For the love of her, is more than anyone else could give to my poor loving heart.

Under my arm was Mercutio slain, therefore in my wrath I slew Tybalt, her cousin. I beg you once more dear father, please forgive me of my sins. For on Earth, I have no place of resting. For Heaven is beckoning to me with a sweet but twisted voice, for in this world no joys can be bestowed to me.

I will hence to the local apothecary and purchase a poison most fatal in effect. Then I shall hasten to Verona, to Juliet's tomb and drink the poison, so I can lie in peace with my lady.

Romeo.

Benjamin Clarke (11)
Bishopsgate School, Egham

Romeo's Last Letter

Dear Father,
　　You shall know that by the time you have read this letter, I will be dead and that I'm begging for forgiveness, as I have gone against your wishes and married a lady by the name of Juliet Capulet. I know that the Capulets are our sworn enemies, but this single soul is enough to make me forget everything that the world has taught me. I have died by her side in the Capulet tomb as I would rather die and be with her, then be living without her. I know you would like to deny this confession that I'm about to make, but it must be spread. It is my fault that Tybalt and Mercutio have been slain. I will rest in peace if this family feud ends. These are my final words.
　　From your loving son,
　　Romeo.

Jamie Sayer (11)
Bishopsgate School, Egham

Beowulf Beats Battling Battleaxes

The past two days have been glorious for our brilliant leader, Beowulf. From the fifteen mighty warriors that set off to Denmark, only two perished. Ivar Fork-Beard was killed during the night of Grendel's death, and Beowulf's best friend, Olaf Longsword, was killed by the hag, Grendel's mother.

We interviewed Beowulf and he revealed how he defeated the monsters.

Beowulf revealed, 'Grendel was easy to beat. After eating Ivar, he reached for me. I grabbed him, and tore his arm off; while fleeing he left his arm behind. He died of blood-loss later that night. We hung Grendel's arm on the wall in the great hall of the Heorot.

When I went to kill the hag, I rode through the dark forest; upon arrival at the pool in the middle of the forest. I jumped into the pool and sank all the way to the bottom, seeing mythical creatures go past.

When I arrived at Grendel's lair, I noticed his body. However, I was attacked by the hag immediately. When I struck at her with my sword, it did not harm her, but her dagger could not penetrate my armour. I then grappled with her, but upon spying a giant cutlass on the wall, I snatched it from the wall and struck at the hag, and killed her'.

Tom Rich (12)
Bishopsgate School, Egham

Man Massacres Monsters

Beowulf brains two nasty beings in the space of two days!

Last night a peculiar series of events unfolded all kick-started when last week Beowulf hacked off the arm of the fearful monster by the name of Grendel, (whose mother is even worse than he is) came to Heorot, in the kingdom of Hrothgar. (The arm is still there if you want a day trip.)

That night (when the watch knight had fallen asleep) Grendel's mother who was even worse than Grendel himself, came and fell on top of one of Beowulf's closest friends and killed him.

So for seven days Beowulf endured blistering winds and scorching desert and he followed Grendel's mother to the deepest and most dark part of the deep, dark woods. Where he found his friend's bleeding head lying next to a stagnant pool.

Beowulf, without fear, put on his armour, picked up his sword ... and sat down for a cup of good old English breakfast tea! His men blew their horns and all the sea snakes and monsters came out but Beowulf didn't mind, he dived in and the old hag grabbed him and pulled him under. It took the best part of nine hours to reach the freezing conditions of the bottom of the pool.

When he and Grendel's mother reached the bottom she dragged him down a slime-ridden corridor to a hall with a roof that kept the water off. There was a fire burning in the hearth and it quickly dried Beowulf out and warmed him up from his long swim down to the bottom.

But brave Beowulf had no time to rest as the hag immediately began to attack him. He picked up his sword and slashed at her but he couldn't cut through her thick hide. So he picked up a giant's cutlass and slammed it into her back and she reeled over in pain.

He quickly cut off Grendel's head as a sign the monster was dead but he left all the other treasures behind.

Meanwhile back on the surface the Danes had left because it had been nine hours and they took Beowulf for dead. But the Goths, who were his own men, stayed until Beowulf emerged, which he did, after eleven hours of waiting. He had brought the head of the fearful monster back up with him. He then had the seven day journey through blistering winds and scorching desert to return to Heorot and his prize was displayed on the wall with the arm of the monster.

James Simcox (12)
Bishopsgate School, Egham

Beowulf The Brave

Just yesterday Beowulf, after having defeated Grendel the monster, yet again took another evil life. This time it was Grendel's mother who was furious about her son's death and wanted revenge.

Beowulf, having sliced off one of Grendel's arms, was unsure of her death as she fled back to her lair. Beowulf chased after her.

At Heorot that night Grendel's mother came to where everyone was sleeping and sliced off the head of one of Beowulf's dearest friends and took it with her.

The next day Beowulf searched for her with the Danes and Goths.

Beowulf's Encounter

Beowulf arrived at a big lake. He knew that at the bottom Grendel would lie. He dived in and found him dead at the bottom of the hall with treasures covering the floors and weapons on the walls. There Grendel was lying on the floor with his mother standing beside him. They both fought until Beowulf grabbed a cutlass off the wall and killed the fiend.

Luke Daines (12)
Bishopsgate School, Egham

He's 'Armless!

In an incredible sting operation, yesterday, when Dr Grendel was doing his rounds, Beowulf, the visiting celebrity, surprised the monster and mortally injured him. The actual details of the clash of warriors are still hazy, but a new piece of modern art, namely a gigantic arm, has attracted a few raised eyebrows over the past few days, after it appeared in King Hrothgar's palace. The Cruelty to Evil Monsters Organisation (CEMO), spoilsports they are, are campaigning for it to be taken down at once.

We interviewed Beowulf at his celebratory feast, last night, he said nonchalantly, 'I couldn't let all my men be ripped limb from limb. One maybe but not all of them! I mean that blood-sucking brute went far enough so I wrestled him!' He went on to say how the very hall shook when he wrenched the thug's arm from the socket!

Another eyewitness stated, 'That thing came down on us like a shark! I started to panic but Beowulf stayed as cool as a polar bear's nostril in a snowstorm!'

Incredible! Beowulf was crowned hero of the year by Hrothgar yesterday.

Horrid Hag Strikes Back!

As we all know yesterday was a time of celebration. However, when we were all snug in our beds, finally free of the oppression of Grendel, Grendel's foul mother snuck into the palace where Beowulf was sleeping, found his best friend, ripped his head off and fled across the moor. An eyewitness stammered, 'She ran like a demon from Hell fleeing a holy man'.

When Beowulf found the bloody remains of his friend, he was filled with rage, he was heard to declare, 'Whether she hides in the dark forest, in the depths of the Earth, or at the bottom of the sea, she will not escape me!' He took a company of men eight hours ago, the Danes have returned but the rest have not been heard from since they marched out of Heorot.

William Locke (12)
Bishopsgate School, Egham

Beowulf The Butcher Is Back

Last week, an implausible event took place. Grendel the fearless monster, who hides away in the treacherous fens beyond the moor, a fiend from Hell, a misbegotten son of a foul mother, came again to Heorot, to feast upon the drunk and stuffed Danes who slumbered around in the great hall.

But earlier in the morning of that day, a youth of valiance who lived far away in the land of the Geats, the mightiest yet mildest of men; his name was Beowulf had heard of the monster's fearless ways of terrorising Heorot and took it as a challenge. He travelled for 40 days and 40 nights, through blizzard conditions in the polar ice caps, to the scorching conditions in the desert, finally to arrive yesterday morning at Heorot, where crowds gathered at his arrival. It was an exciting day for everyone as they had heard of Beowulf and his amazing skills with the sword.

As the sun fell from the sky and the moon rose, fear stank in the walls of Heorot. Beowulf took off his armour, sheathed his sword and laid down beside his bed, closed his eyes and waited. There was deep silence and then suddenly a slight crunch sound, and then a bang on the door, and then another and another. The monster lifted the door off its hinges before the wood splintered and the door flew down. Everyone stayed perfectly still and the breath of the monster stunk out the room.

Grendel grabbed a slave from his bed and, before he'd even had a chance to scream, tore him apart limb from limb. Greedily the monster grabbed for another, but as he bent down, Beowulf sprang up from his bed, pulled his sword out of its sheath and swung at Grendel. Beowulf cut straight through his shoulder blade and blood spurted out everywhere.

Grendel roared with pain, turned around, picked up Beowulf and threw him to the other side of the room, before stumbling back into the depths of the forest. Beowulf stood up and then told his men to follow the monster and to make sure it did not return.

There still wasn't much sign of celebration, as the monster was not dead and so the fear of him coming back was high.

But this morning anxiety was upon everyone, celebration for the foreigner, Beowulf, he came and saved us all from Grendel the gruesome monster!

Beowulf says he is going to remain in Heorot in case the monster does come back, but he did say that it is very unlikely the monster will.

In the great hall of Heorot displayed his prize, the massive arm of Grendel himself!

George Irons (12)
Bishopsgate School, Egham

Gory Grendel Meets His Match

An incredible incident occurred last night that will be remembered for centuries. Last night, Beowulf set up a sting operation so that he could trap Grendel, the evil monster, in Heorot in the kingdom of Hrothgar.

Grendel eventually came to the hall, bringing his appetite with him. As he ripped the door from its hinges, threw it to one side and entered, he scanned the room. He pounced on the nearest soldier, tore him limb from limb and swallowed him whole, sucking the blood in streams and munching on the bones. Half-gorged, his foul appetite still unslaked, he then laid his demon-like eyes on Beowulf and Beowulf laid his eyes on Grendel. They stared at each other, then Grendel sprang forwards towards Beowulf and they tussled. They threw each other about the room and the building's foundations shook. Next, Beowulf tore Grendel's arm from his shoulder, wrenched it from the root while the tough sinews snapped. The monster let out a mighty howl, well knowing that would end his fiendish days.

Grendel fled from Hrothgar and back to his cave, spilling blood wherever he went. Grendel then died.

But back in Hrothgar, Beowulf rejoiced in his victory and held his blood-soaked prize high. Beowulf kept this arm as a trophy. Grendel's massive arm was pinned to the wall, its nails made of jagged steel and brutal spikes. Beowulf celebrated and told everyone the next morning.

Old Hag Retaliates After Son's Death

After Grendel, the monster, died last night, his mother, the old hag, came into Heorot, in the kingdom of Hrothgar, and killed Beowulf's best friend. Beowulf will set out to find the hag tomorrow.

Here we have an eyewitness account of the murder. Here we have Smelly Sven. 'So Sven, what did you hear, smell and see?'

'Well, first I heard the loud crack of wood and I saw that the door had been torn open. It's a shame really, I fixed that door right after Grendel came today. Now I have to do it all over again. Anyway, then I smelt the worst smell I've smelt in me life, and me uncle is Flatulent Frank. He died last night, turns out he got a hernia trying to push out a fart. Poor man ...'

'I'm sorry folks the interview is taking too long. You'll hear from me next time on The Danes' Drivel. Bye'.

Jack Lowe (12)
Bishopsgate School, Egham

Autobiography Of Anneke Klays

This is my story, the story of me, the story of my life. This story is different, my story is unusual, my story is dangerous.

My name is Anneke Gretchen Erica Klays; I was born in Otz in Austria, right at the tip of the Alps. My birth date is the 17th May 1933.

My mother's name is Erica Monica Klays; there is no need to state my father's name as he is not important now. From the day I was born my mother knew my life had changed forever and it has.

On the 17th May 1933 a crisis broke out. It was everywhere: 'Mount Hochberg opens its doors and lets off a little weight'. Otz, a small village at the foot of the Hochberg was covered. Only the very few who survived the tremors and shakes, who then fled to the safest hiding point lived to tell the tale. I was one of those very few.

It was a magical night when I first opened my eyes to the world. But then the night was destroyed, the memory lost, locked up in a black chest not to be opened until now.

The house shook that night. My father ran out of the wooden house and saw men running, women crying, children scared to death. A rampaging avalanche was gushing down from the tip of Mount Hochberg.

From then on all I know is that somehow me and my just given-birth mother managed to escape to a nearby town. My father never came with us, I don't know why. How we escaped I don't know. It seems hard to believe, I find it hard to believe. But it's true. It's a miracle really.

Rhiannon Pratt (11)
George Abbot School, Guildford

The Flower Vase Princess

Once upon a time in a land far away a beautiful girl was born called Princess Jasmine. She had ebony hair and a crowd of adorers. She was born in King Bernard's castle. King Bernard had a lovely wife called Henrietta and they loved each other very much.

But a witch, called Hazel, who had dingy hair and a blotchy nose, arrived at the castle to ruin the christening and put an evil spell on the baby so she would turn into a flower vase at sunset and become herself at sunrise. Only a handsome prince could break the spell.

One morning as Jasmine came down to breakfast, King Bernard asked, 'Would you like to go to the market for a pet?'

'Oh yes please!' she answered. 'I'd love to!'

So they went down to market.

That evening, as the princess was about to change into her flower vase, the pet guinea pig squeaked, 'Please kiss me, I'm the Prince of Far Away and you shall break the spell if you kiss me!'

'Who's that?' she asked.

'Your guinea pig!' the prince replied. 'I'll give you something in return for setting me free!'

'OK, but hurry, I'm changing into a flower vase!'

The guinea pig jumped to her and she kissed him. Just in time because then the princess vanished and a flower vase replaced her.

The prince, who was himself again, was almost crying with happiness at being set free from the enchantment that had cursed him for years. He waited until morning and when the princess was back as a princess, he kissed her and her spell broke. The prince asked Jasmine's parents whether he could marry her and they said that he could and they all lived happily ever after.

You may wonder what happened to the witch. She was caught trying to poison their wedding meal …

Elizabeth Hogg (12)
George Abbot School, Guildford

The Beginning

She walked down the street, it was sunset. Her long black hair trailed behind her and her old white dress clung to her dead, limp body. She smiled, it would soon be time. People were staring, screaming, pointing. But there was nothing she could do - yet. Soon they would bow to her, as if she were a god.

She came to the forest and walked through with not a care in the world. There it was, ahead of her, what she was waiting for.

In front of her was the Cindanay, the most beautiful weapon in the world. She stepped forward, smiling, her evil smile. She uttered four words no one else could hear and then it began, from everywhere things were awakening, dead things, dark things. They were drawn to her, longing for her. Her army. It was time …

Megan Barber (12)
George Abbot School, Guildford

Bang!

As I was trying to get my boots on and my laces tied the air raid siren went off like a giant wasp ready to sting. I grabbed my teddy and my little sister's hand and ran as fast as I could to the air raid shelter. Mum shortly joined us holding the cat in one hand and a letter from Dad in the other. My dad is in the RAF now.

The air raid finished and we went to the train station, we were going to Scotland to stay at Auntie Bettie's house until the war dies down and Dad returned. Things will be a lot different when we come back from Scotland; buildings will be destroyed, family and friends might go missing and later turn up under a pile of bricks.

The train eventually came, the musty smell of smoke rose to my nose and the loud hooting of the train's engine bellowed in my ears. We opened the train door, stepped in, trying to miss the huge gap between the platform and train floor, the bottom end of my suitcase got stuck under the seat. My mum called me to the window and gave me a hankie, I held it out the window as we started to move, the wind blew against the hankie. On the platform Mum waved, saying goodbye!

Rebekah Smith (12)
George Abbot School, Guildford

War

Thomas stumbled through the thick and dense trees of the forest until he came across a village. The ground was damp and wet. The houses were made of wood and had thatched roofs. Thomas had archers ready to defend the village because he knew his cousin was coming to find him.

Suddenly he heard hooves from the trees he just came from, the ground started shaking, the noise got louder and louder, some of the leaves fell off the trees. Thomas shouted at his archers to get in formation behind the bushes near the forest. Thomas got out his broad head arrow to bring down the horses, he put the arrow on the bow getting ready to loosen. All of his archers got out their broad head arrows ready to loosen.

The noise of hooves stopped for a heartbeat. Then *twang,* a bunch of arrows hit Thomas' men. Thomas loosened his arrow. It caught the wind and imbedded itself in an archer's neck. He loosened another. The second arrow went through one of the enemies' mouths and took off his skull. Thomas was about to put an arrow on the bow when he dropped it. He was about to pick it off the floor, when an arrow hit Thomas in the neck. Blood covered Thomas' bow, he went stone cold, another arrow hit Thomas in the back and broke Thomas' spine. Then he collapsed on the floor … *dead!*

Fergus Bell (12)
George Abbot School, Guildford

Army Of The Night

Eyes aflame, she stood before her army of the night, raven hair streaming in the wind, skin hanging lifeless and limp off her skeletal body, her sordid midnight dress flapping in the night. Upon her lips played a devilish smile. She showed her stiletto fangs and addressed her army, 'Tonight we feast and the land will run crimson with the blood of man.'

The legions erupted in roars of delight. Soon the last screams of Man would fill the night and a red sky would rise on the morrow.

They stood there, waiting for the inevitable, cloaked in silence and armed with grim crossbows and merciless swords, clad in silver they waited. They were not afraid, for there were worst punishments than death. They prayed they would die rather than endure the hellish existence of the legions of the damned.

In the distance they could hear the onslaught on many clothed feet. Their hearts beat as one with those shadow footsteps. Before the army stood the king, eyes grim and set, he would save this land or die in the process, for life was no life in the shadow of such evil.

Still the approaching army came ever closer, till suddenly they stopped and a shadowy figure alighted to the ground. A single command uttered from her ebony lips, 'Charge.'

It had begun.

Hannah Blackwood (14)
George Abbot School, Guildford

Spooky Forest

I ventured into the forest not daring to picture what might live in its shadowy branches. Still sticking to the path I wandered deeper, deeper into the wilderness. I could hear a faint screaming in the distance.

I stopped and clenched my sword, I had heard something stir amongst the ancient leaves. Was it merely a rat, or maybe two? I was now staring at a whole rat army and they didn't look too happy. I wondered what to do, whether I should run or fight. What I saw next made my mind up, for coming towards me were two vicious giant rats!

I started to run and I kept on running until I reached a clearing. I cautiously prowled around until I discovered a huge footprint. It was human-shaped but it only had four toes. I suddenly realised that something was breathing down my neck. I whipped around only to look into the face of a fully grown giant! *Bang!* was the last thing I ever heard for I had just stumbled upon a giant's den.

'It's my turn, it's my turn,' screamed my little brother. 'It's my go on the new game!'

Ritchie Lord (12)
George Abbot School, Guildford

War Story

Bang, crash! Clatter, clatter, splash! A great cheering erupted from the deck of our ship, but it was very short-lived. Another German Stuka was bearing down on us. As we tried to shoot it down with our machine guns we noticed it showed no sign of pulling up out of its ear-splitting dive. It was now close enough to see the pilot and he looked crazed! The Stuka crashed into the deck with a deafening crack! After the splintered wood and the dust had been blown away we approached the Stuka very cautiously. The pilot and the gunner were certainly dead. You could tell as the pilot and the gunner were covered by screens of blood in the cockpit.

Suddenly someone shouted, 'It's still got a bomb attached!' Everyone stopped dead in their tracks and backed away to the railing on the side of the ship. None of us cared what was happening all around us and neither did any of us turn our head when we saw a supply tanker capsized a few metres away. Our mission was to protect the cargo ships till they reached Malta. Without these supplies the entire Allied North American campaign would be wrecked.

One of our two bomb defusers stepped forward to disarm the bomb. 'I need a volunteer to help me try this thing,' said Freddy Jones (he was the bomb defuser). I found myself volunteering without a second thought. 'OK, let's get cracking,' he said.

It took us a few minutes but soon we had disarmed the bomb and heaved it into the water. It was only then everything became much more relaxed about what had happened. We surveyed the damage that had been done. Our losses were light and there still were a few German ships retreating. *Kaboom!* There went another German Z1. We all laughed about it afterwards.

I never stopped shaking until we arrived at the port.

William James (12)
George Abbot School, Guildford

Outnumbered

I woke up to find my head hurt badly. I was a long way from base camp and all I could see were scattered bodies and vehicles gutted by fire. I got up to see if any of my comrades were still alive, I didn't find any until a moment later when I heard a moaning sound coming from one of the machine-gun nests. I rushed over and helped him up to find his leg had been badly wounded. I got a bandage out of my first-aid kit and wrapped it around his leg. I tried a radio that was around someone's waist but there was no signal. I cursed under my breath and we started to pick up guns and ammo. It was a long way back to base camp and we didn't know what or who we would bump into.

We staggered through the abyss in the direction of base camp, hoping that we would get past the army heading for our base camp. I took out my binoculars and compass and looked in the direction of base camp. We then saw the most gut-squeezing sight we had ever seen. The army had turned around and were heading back. I called for John as I'd learnt his name to be, and we ran to the nearest sand dune and quickly planned a new route around the army of 30. One slight noise and we would be dead meat ...

Sam Jewell (11)
George Abbot School, Guildford

War And Death

I was in pain, my whole arm in agony. I needed urgent care, immediately. But it was impossible from the position I was in. I was in the centre of the battlefield, people dying in front of me, just impossible. I needed to fight, fight my way through the harsh battlefield to find a medic. I had an AK47 on my free arm, I had to use this to help me kill the Germans. It was a heavy gun but I had to cope.

I saw a man in front of me screaming as a bullet shot through his body, it was a horrific and bloody scene. It was amazing how much blood could flood through such a small hole. The German shot more bullets through my teammate with a machine gun and he fell dead in front of me. I shouted, 'Noooo!' and with my one hand shot as many bullets as I could through the AK47 into the German's head. He fell headless on the ground with blood shooting out of his neck.

I had no time to realise that for the first time ever I'd killed a man. Instead I started running to the small hospital with a dead arm beside me, killing people as I ran.

I took a quick glimpse in front of me, I saw a German hidden behind bunkers of sand with a 50 cal aimed at me. I shouted loudly, 'Please don't kill me!' but the German showed no mercy at all.

Lloyd Stephens (11)
George Abbot School, Guildford

My Machine

I could feel the dusty breeze as it swept up a pile of soot. A carpet of dust lay down before me. Circular patterns of ice and frost had been pasted on a cracked-looking glass. Marbled stains were thrust into a rough turquoise rug, abandoned belongings had been cascaded onto the cracked concrete. Sirens were dead and there was no signal from a smashed radio. Crumbs of tasty food were left moulding whilst a dripping noise came from a lonely standing heater. Flames crackled and I was ready for an explosion. I turned on the sucking machine ready to duck. It was me against a battle between survival and death.

Oh my word! Me and my dreaded Hoover, ready to clean this bombsite of my bedroom!

Katie Butchers (12)
George Abbot School, Guildford

A Day In The Life Of Peter Nagel

I wake up to the sound of ... nothing. This house is always silent. All my grandfather does is sit in his study all day, but today, because he is a doctor, he has to go and visit a patient, so after breakfast I am free to roam around this vast, echoing house, the first time in about a year. I don't need to look upstairs, I did that when everyone had gone to sleep about a month ago, and it had been a disappointment. All it had consisted of were 7 bedrooms, all empty except for mine and Grandfather's rooms, which, even then, only had a wardrobe and a small single bed.

The first room I walk in to is the dining room. I know this room, but I've never been through the door at the other end of this vast room. I turn the gold handle, push back the heavy oak door. It leads into the library, which I am forbidden to enter.

Cautiously I put one foot over the threshold. Rows and rows of books as far as the eye can see, but what catches my eye the most is the red door at the other end of this cosy room. It is my grandfather's study. There is a wide dark desk at the window. I'd seen this from the back garden a few days before whilst playing football. There are three towering bookshelves. One shelf is lined with big bottles; inside there are what seems to be floating dolls.

I take another step, cautiously, into this eerie room. Fräulein Strecker's (my maths tutor) painting of a parakeet hangs right next to the door. I take another step and then another till I am right inside this room - the room I am not allowed in. I walk over to the desk and I pull open a drawer. It is filled to the brim with letters from my father to my grandfather and it is here I spend the rest of the afternoon reading through the past year of my father's life.

Amy Danilewicz (12)
George Abbot School, Guildford

A Wartime Promise
(An extract)

From war to the country

Her face pressed up against the window, causing a fog to mist it over. She was saddened by the thought of her father going into war, fearing his death and her family's grief. The tears couldn't be held back any longer, she plunged herself into a bundle on the floor, weeping and sobbing. Her dress draped around her, the lace dried her tears but they just kept coming.

The youngest of all the three children, Emily entered the room. She threw her arms around Florence to reassure her. 'Mother said he will be back before we know it. We just need to be patient and pray to God. That's what she said anyway.'

'Oh I know dear Emily, but it does not stop it from hurting any less does it?'

'Indeed not. But we all are suffering, even Mother.'

Florence picked herself up and headed downstairs where she saw her mother, Mary, packing their bags. She wore a one-piece siren suit and carried her largish handbag which contained the family ration book.

Her mother walked over to her and wiped her face, gently kissing her forehead. 'We must all be strong and hold back our tears. Your father has gone to fight for us, for the country and for him. He will be back, I promise you that, but for now we must move to the country in the unfortunate event that the sirens sound and the enemy attacks. You are all far too young to understand, so just trust me and we will be safe.' She moved back over to the sacks where she was packing up all the family's belongings ready for our stay in the country. She was just as scared as the children but she had to be strong for both herself and her children's state of mind.

The second eldest child was Edward, the man of the family as of now. He wore just ordinary trousers with a plain T-shirt and hair gelled. He picked up both his and his little sister Emily's sacks and led the way to the train station, wiping back the tears as he walked. Florence carried Emily and Mary carried her own sack, food and a brave face.

They waited at the station and watched many other families of mothers and children arrive in their hundreds. The train came in with a screech and the children started to board. Mary lifted the sacks on and slammed the door of the carriage, shutting out her entire past life. The children read books whilst Mary just sat, looking out the window and silently crying.

'Mother are you alright?' Edward grabbed his mother's hand as Florence nudged him to comfort her.

'I am perfectly splendid thank you, just a little emotional about leaving my home just as you three are about leaving your father.'

Silence was established again. No one spoke until Emily started to sing her father's favourite song. Every word she sung, the others mimed and cheerfully smiled along with droplets of tears. They started to hit their thighs and boosted moral throughout the cabin.

Rachel Price (13)
Haling Manor High School, South Croydon

Clarinet Dream

The day I went was the day when my life was reborn.

I woke from a dark life, no colour was repeated in this life just a repetition of shadows. The way I woke was like a fairy tale; my hero shone and its voice came out like many emotional tones. No, not a knight in shining armour but a clarinet.

There was no musician handling the keys that shone like the sun viewed by mankind. It played a tune that no person could have kept up with, but for a strange reason I could feel the tune vibrating on my nerve endings, making hairs stand to attention.

There was jazz, opera, soul and a hint of improvisation. As my eyes started to focus, I could see my surroundings, it was like a million instruments in all different positions starting to make a masterpiece for the future. There were cellos, trumpets, guitars and more clarinets. There was one problem with all the instruments the cellos and guitars had no strings. The clarinets had no reeds and the trumpets had no mouthpieces. But then they all unjumbled and stood against the wall like a call up. Then I started to wonder about an imaginary world of things that didn't even involve the ordinary world.

The clarinet started to play more of its low but moving music. It seemed that all the other musical instruments were obsessed with the clarinet's music.

I was now confused, what could the musical instruments hear that I couldn't?

Lilly Emeney (13)
Horndean Technology College, Waterlooville

The Poison Of Riches
(An extract)

Her head was banging, her stomach swirling, she thought she was going to throw up. *How could this happen?* she thought. Before she could stop herself, tears were squeezing out of her eyes. Her house, her lovely, lovely house would be taken, she'd have to sell her wonderful designer clothes, she wouldn't get that cruise ... It was all her dad's fault; he was the one that wanted to sell the company that had made Isabella's family so rich and famous! His deal fell through and now he had lost the family everything. Isabella Harvey and her family had gone bankrupt!

But Issy had a plan; she wouldn't lower herself to being middle-class! She already knew that Richard Brewer - the village doctor and now richest available man - was after her.

The next day, news spread fast around the sleepy old village of Brooksfield that Isabella Harvey and Richard Brewer were 'shock, horror' engaged to be married!

The ceremony was simple yet elegant ... Well, Issy knew that she had to look stunning at her wedding even though she didn't care for Richard. She hovered by the champagne table, looking cautiously around. It was now or never. She had already made her husband make a new will and take out life insurance, all she needed to do now was make sure that it wouldn't take too long for the money to come through ...

'Darling, have some wine! Celebrate!' Issy offered her husband a drink. *Well, you'll have to celebrate now, there won't be time later!* she added secretly inside her head. All of a sudden the new groom's breathing started to slow down, his heart stopping and head spinning.

'Help, help,' Richard croaked quietly.

Oh no, it wasn't supposed to be as blatant as this! He could at least die quietly! Issy thought to herself selfishly.

As Richard keeled over he commanded a crowd of family and friends. He took his last breath silently. His life was over before it had begun. His aunt ran over to him, she knew the signs, he had been poisoned, and she wasn't going to let the murderer get away with it!

Once the groom's body had been taken away, the police called and the area was sealed off, Miss Marple decided to introduce herself to the widow. Her nephew's wife ...

Samantha Leimanis (12)
Horndean Technology College, Waterlooville

Hop, Skip And Jump

As I stumble to the edge, my nerves collapse at my feet, frayed, worn and broken. Though my shell is still, my insides have long fallen in, a constant melee in my emotions. Fear fights with my courage, depression stakes the heart of my wilting optimism. Who do they think they're staring at? I'm not as crazy as they think I am. Why don't I let them cry on my shoes? Maybe then we can sing the same tune. All together now ... 'One, two, three, hop, skip ... jump.'

Don't bother with the safety net, and don't you dare call the police. Put away your cameras and hide your worried faces and, just for me, paint on a face of counterfeit happiness. After all; I'll have gone to a better place, won't I? Just sit back and watch the performance of my public disaster. Put down your pens and quit writing your tragedies. Let me slip into the limelight and fall.

Now forget your anguish, and read my final scrawls. Just remember and take heed. Slit wrists are just a fashion statement so ... why not join me in the game where we play God. Let's show the world we're serious. For the secret to immortality is to live a life that will be remembered or, to die a death that won't be clean forgot. But, may I remind you: falling feels like flying, until you hit the ground.

Lorna Salmon (14)
Horndean Technology College, Waterlooville

The Alleyway

Tricia Dent was 14. The night in question, October 15th 1989. She had moved to this secluded town about 3 weeks earlier and already she had learnt of one place to stay away from. The alleyway that led from the shops to the street her new house was in. There were stories about this alleyway but the one that seemed to be the most reliable went like this ...

According to legend a young boy (about your age, the locals would say) was found in that very alleyway strangled and badly beaten on October 15th 1889 and that on that night every 100 years his ghost came, seeking a victim just as his murderer did. Her stepdad had dismissed these stories as crazy rumours used to scare children. Now, she was not worried to use the alleyway because she was late coming home from a friend's and decided to cut through to save time.

Although she didn't believe the story, it didn't stop her being scared and she sped up. Her hurried footsteps echoed off the mossy walls and were very slowly joined by the sound of struggled breathing. She spun round and saw the boy's ghost slowly shuffling up the alleyway towards her with its arms outstretched. The next thing she knew it was strangling her with one arm while the other hit her.

The police found her body next morning strangled and badly beaten. Her stepdad was found in the house 3 days later hung by Tricia's school tie.

Kayleigh Robins (14)
Horndean Technology College, Waterlooville

A Day In The Life Of An Ant

Dear Diary,

Today has been so exhausting! First, this human thinks that it is funny to poke a stick into our colony and make us run everywhere. Then another human tries to swat us with that square thing with holes in it. Well, the human was saying that ants were disgusting creatures! What is wrong with an ant? I mean, we are not slimy or anything. Personally, I think that humans are more disgusting than ants.

Also, another thing that happened was that our hill sprang a leak. Remember when I said that a human poked a stick into our colony? Well, the stick made a hole in our hill and then it started to rain. So every single ant had to try and stop the leak, get rid of the water (somehow) and keep the hill dry from mossing over.

Well, I must be getting back to work because the boss is starting to get moody.

Anthony Ant.

Hannah Watson (12)
Horndean Technology College, Waterlooville

Which Way Now? - A Tale Of Two Halves

Lying in that cold and desolate crevasse, alone, with no contact with seemingly another world, to me felt amazing. I couldn't believe I was alive! As I plummeted down that mountain, the razor-sharp, icy wind burning at my face, I truly believed that was it; I was dead. As I hit the hard, frozen floor, my heart skipped a beat and I had to compose myself gulping for precious air. I could feel I'd broken a leg on landing, but surprisingly it wasn't hurting and I felt refreshed and prepared; but for what? I knew Simon must have released the rope and my mind froze picturing him alone above. We'd vowed to be strong until becoming too frail and I knew the trip had been a strain. Heart pounding, I had to find him.

I collapsed into the snow, but it didn't give way under my weight; it was frozen. Every muscle in my body tremored from the impact and warm tears flowing from my eyes quickly solidified, but I didn't wipe them away before they stuck to my face; I felt ashamed. How could I tell anyone what I'd done, whilst how could I leave with the slim chance he'd made it? He was doomed if I left it this way, but could I save him now? There was only one thing to do and the risk was huge. I prepared appropriately, as if just setting out, beginning the downhill climb that could lead to both our ends …

Lisa-Jayne Wiseman (14)
Horndean Technology College, Waterlooville

No Escape

Teeth, snow-white, gleamed at me bearing an evil grin; cold eyes bore into my soul freezing my heart. She strode forward and seized my arm; her extensive nails pinched my frail skin. She gave a wicked smirk and reached forwards to whisper in my ear. I flinched as her glossy black hair brushed against my pale face making my skin crawl. Her sneering voice reduced to a hiss and crept into every segment of my body.

'You can run, but you can't hide.'

She hit me hard in the chest; I doubled up in pain and fell to the floor gritting my teeth in agony. From the corner of my eye I could see her standing casually with a smile on her face suggesting she was amused. After several minutes she nonchalantly strolled forward, bending down beside me. Suddenly she seized a clump of hair pulling me upwards. I bit my tongue to stop myself screaming. Tears streamed down my blemished face as she shook my head to face hers.

'Please stop. Please!' I whimpered.

'I'll never stop! I won't rest until you're a crumpled mess!' she screamed with laughter.

I now thought she was mad. Her eyes were bulging dangerously, flecks of spit drooled down her laughing mouth.

'There's no escape.'

She kicked me hard and suddenly I was falling.

A violent jolt woke me to find my sheets drenched in sweat and my heart hammering against my chest. I realised she was out there. Waiting for me …

Kirsty Claridge (14)
Horndean Technology College, Waterlooville

One Day In The Life Of Trampus

My master never fed me. He came downstairs into the kitchen and took me for a walk on my lead.

I ran off. Master came after me, I never came back for him.

Pet Rescue took me away from Master. He came to Pet Rescue to take me away, but I hid from him. I stayed at Pet Rescue all night. Perhaps I will find a new home with a master who will feed me.

Simon Thomas (15)
Limington House School, Basingstoke

The Image

Chloe stared at her feet. In her head she could still see the hearse driving past and the flowery letters spelling 'Mum' on the back of the coffin. She looked up as the wind blew her chocolate curls into her face. The park in front of her lay deserted. The climbing frame had been vandalised and the swing had been snapped. As Chloe looked at the sandpit she remembered her mum and a tear trickled down her face.

Rain smeared Chloe's mascara as she walked home. As soon as she stepped into her room she took a chest from under her bed and removed a small linen-covered album from it. A picture of her mum flickered on every page. She came to a picture that had been taken ten seconds before a bullet had pierced her mum's heart. Then she stopped; a tall, dark figure, who she recognised, stood with a gun. Taking a pistol from her sock drawer she sprinted downstairs.

Her uncle lay on the couch. Chloe aimed the pistol at him. 'Murderer!' she screamed and slowly squeezed the trigger.

Jordan Knight (12)
Mayville High School, Southsea

The Race

It was school sports day. Thirteen-year-old Jessica won every year without fail. She was the sportiest in the school. Jess' toughest challenge was still to come. She dreamt of winning the Olympics.

Vince was the toughest boy in school. He was always jealous of Jess, constantly trying to beat her, but ended up humiliating himself. Whenever he heard Jessica's name, rage would bubble up inside him. He wanted to take revenge.

Vince arranged for a race between him and Jess. He had been thinking, his plan of revenge was simple.

'Jess' class is on the top floor. She is always in a rush, so all I have to do is to push her down the stairs. That way she will injure herself and not be able to run as fast or she will have to forfeit the game, meaning I win!' whispered Vince proudly to Mike, his best mate.

The next morning Vince put his plan into action. Mike pushed Jess just as she was going down. *Crash!* Jess fell injuring her leg. She was taken to hospital. Vince looked worried. He had just realised what he had done; something so terrible. She was already hurt, there was nothing he could do about that, but there was still the race.

The playground was packed, everyone was waiting for the race. Jess was nowhere in sight.

'It looks like Jess has forfei …'

'There she is!' the crowd roared.

As the crowd went silent Vince stood up and said in a loud voice, *'I forfeit the race, Jessica wins!'*

Zahra Jaffer (11)
Mayville High School, Southsea

A Day In The Life Of Scrappy!

I am Scrappy. I was abandoned by my owner last Christmas. After that I lived in half of an old shed in a dump. I think it was about two or three days ago my life finally changed, whether it is a good thing or a bad thing I cannot say, anyway not at this point in time.

It all started when I was going through Tensen Street like any normal day searching for my daily breakfast. Well, at number 37 they had leftover chicken on Wednesday. Number 37's dumpster was my favourite place to eat. Anyway, what I didn't know was that an old lady lived there and she didn't much like dogs; actually she didn't much like any sort of animal to be honest.

Well she called the dog pound. Man's best friend is supposed to be a dog, but with these dog catchers, this is a different case.

He came, I ran. I ran as fast as I could but he cornered me in a bashed down alley. My heart was beating as fast as lightning hits the ground. My home now is a cold, damp, small cage; all you can hear is the sound of other dogs howling. I am scared, very scared. All I ever wanted was someone to love me.

Elisabeth Welfare (12)
Mayville High School, Southsea

A Day In The Life Of A Child In Uganda

I live in Uganda in a small town called Soroti. I am the second youngest child in my family. Every day my two brothers Mohammed and Gulam go to school. The school has a thatched roof and the tables and chairs are made of cane, beautifully crafted and handmade. My sister stays home with my mum as she is only young. My mum has a very special talent in dressmaking and she makes me some exquisite clothes. They are very trendy and really comfortable. We have a servant who is very kind and tolerant and he does all the washing, cleaning, ironing; helps my mum with the cooking and many more things.

My dad runs a clothes shop. Today as usual I had come to the shop to help him. It's really exciting as my dad lets me serve the customers and talk to them. One of my tasks for today is to open up the new stock of materials that has come in. They are very colourful and vibrant. I stack the last of the material on the neat pile and skip off to the front of the shop where my dad is waiting for me to go home.

When we get home he sits me on his knee and tells me a story about all the exciting things he did when he was young and he always teaches me something new and interesting.

Sayyeda-Maryam Gangji (12)
Mayville High School, Southsea

I Looked Death In The Face

My name is Pat Davis and I've died. Well, only for a minute. It was the 8th April and I'd given birth to my son, Guy, three days earlier. I was still in hospital.

It was a normal day. My husband Frank had brought me fresh orange juice. I remember going to sleep. Then I heard a tap on the glass above my door. I looked over to the door and saw the window above was half open. I don't know how I managed it, I was able to see straight through the door. Standing there were six men dressed in clothes from different periods in time; Edwardian, Tudor and so on.

They said to me, 'Pat, come with us!'

I replied, 'If I'm chained to the bed then I'll go, but if I'm not I'll stay here, because it means they trust me not to leave!' I picked up the covers of my bed and I saw no chains. So I declared, 'I'll not come with you today!'

I later learned I died for a minute in my sleep, but the doctors had brought be back.

The next morning Frank came in to visit. The matron stopped him to say, 'I'm sorry Mr Davis.'

At this point my husband's heart froze, thinking the worst.

'Your father, James Davis, died earlier this morning. We are very sorry.'

James Davis, my father-in-law, was taken instead of me.

It is a day I've never forgotten.

Victoria O'Brien (12)
Mayville High School, Southsea

Amazing!

Monkey World has cracked it. Now there's a new way to carry out medical checks on the monkeys without using drugs. It's a much safer way for both the monkeys and the keepers. The monkeys wait for a bell when they can stop to get a reward of fruit juice.

We spoke to keeper, Jeremy, who has started the training. He said, 'I'm very pleased it's going so well. Not having to drug the monkeys, makes it far less stressful for them'.

Maybe other zoos will try it out. The training lessons teach the monkeys to reply to simple commands such as: 'show me your tummy'. This also shows that monkeys are as intelligent as people say they are.

Georgina Cullen (11)
Mayville High School, Southsea

A Day In The Life Of ...

A day in the life of me! Sadie Banks! You have got to be kidding. Jeez, you don't know what you've let yourself in for. I'm a fourteen-year-old female who lives in this grotty old orphanage. That's right; I'm an orphan. Well, not exactly an orphan, but that's what it feels like.

You see my mum had me when she was sixteen and now here I am! So I guess you could call it a home for parentless children. You guys don't know how lucky you are to have parents, and no, I'm not insane; I do know what I'm talking about.

I'm choosing my options in school this year. Before I know it, I'll be in college. That's why I'm planning on finding her. My mum, that is. I know she misses me; she must do, mustn't she? I miss her and I can't even remember what she sounds like - let alone looks like!

I just want to know what it feels like to love someone and be loved back. The only thing that's ever meant anything to me was Ug, and he was my pet woodlouse, when I was three. So you see what I mean?

Everyone here keeps telling me it's not possible to 'track her down', including the people that work here. I'm supposed to be at school right now. If they can't be bothered to help me, then I can't be bothered to go to school! So I guess it's up to me to find her!

Eliza Castleton (12)
Mayville High School, Southsea

Loss

Whoosh! The sound of the waves crashing onto the shore was like music. Of course though I wasn't like the seals jumping in. I couldn't swim, was the runt of the herd, the one to be pushed around. My 'mum' defended me though, she didn't care that I was different, she knew the real me.

I walked off, saw a shiny metal object. I looked into it and saw an Arctic fox! I ran for my life back to the herd and saw some more coming! I pounced on something coming towards me, too scared to open my eyes. It had stopped struggling, I gathered all the courage I had to look and I jumped. It was my mum …

It was a mirror I had looked into. I was part of the fox skulk, left for dead by nature. I had turned on the one that really loved me. I'd never see her again. She was gone. Forever.

Soraya Al-Mahrouq (13)
Mayville High School, Southsea

Dragon Slayer

In a circle of fire we see that a warrior, very tall, with searing red eyes that you can see through the visor of his helmet, is armed head to toe in steel armour and wielding two swords as if they were attached to his arms. He is fighting a fierce black dragon with a menacing forked tongue that flicks out from his sinister snarl. With an evil roar he spits an enormous ball of fire at the warrior. As fast as lightning the warrior avoids the searing ball of fire and before the dragon can think of another move, the warrior impales his right sword through the dragon's head. The dragon squeals in pain and falls to the floor, dead!

The warrior, still holding the sword that inflicted the death blow begins to chant in a strange language, 'May you merge with the flames from Hell, skin to metal, flesh to sword, to make the metal of fire, for I am Damien.' As soon as these words have been spoken, the dragon turns into a large metal box, with a dragon scale pattern that gives the appearance of being carved into it. Damien tries to open it, but he can't. The box appears to be sealed by a strong, mysterious force.

James MacFarlane (13)
Mayville High School, Southsea

Dragons In The Night

It was a cold, soulless night. The only thing heard from people's windows was singing from the local pub and the crashing of bins as bears searched for scraps of food. A reptilian was silhouetted against the moon with a wingspan of 100 feet. An old man left the pub, he was about 6ft 10 wearing a brown coat, scarf and bowler hat. The scarf covered most of his face with only the eyes and forehead showing. He quickened his pace so as to get home to his family. As if out of nowhere another reptilian was silhouetted against the moon. Of course the man couldn't see this because his back was facing them. 'Damn this cold weather,' he said as the reptilian came in for the kill and *splat*, there was blood everywhere as the reptilians ripped him in half. He was never seen again.

After that there was no noise, the street was quiet and even the bears had stopped. The street was deserted, more like a ghost town than a city. The only noise heard that night was the inhumane sound of a dragon and the whistle of the wind through the trees.

The next day everything was still. Offices and schools were closed, cars in garages, everyone looking out of their windows, waiting for the next victim of the dragons. It would be mating season next month and everyone knew that they would have to move to a different city or die.

Jacques Voller (12)
Mayville High School, Southsea

Night Falls On The City

The streets are deserted. The smell of dead rats lingers in the air turning away anybody who comes close. The only sound to be heard are those of owls. The silhouettes of birds can be seen crossing the moonlit sky. Then suddenly a rattling sound comes from a bin in the distance. It begins to topple slightly. After much swaying it crashes to the ground and out dives a small girl holding a brown rotten apple core. Quickly munching it, she continues limping down the road in her tattered socks.

Her clothes are torn and filthy. She has nothing to keep her warm. Her height suggests that she is about eight. She finishes eating and tosses away the stalk making her face visible. It is covered in dust and soot. But her eyes explain everything. The eyes tell stories of what she has seen. These things include murder and rape. The eyes tell stories of her hopes. Hopes of finding a caring man who will pay to keep her looked after and well fed. Hopes of a man who will send her to school for an education. The eyes also tell stories of her fears. Fears of being abducted and kept as a hostage. Fears of dying alone on the streets, nobody knowing she's ever existed. But she has no time to wait and think about the future as she hurriedly searches for bins, sees none and continues her helpless limp down the long road and into the darkness.

Tom Petty (11)
Mayville High School, Southsea

Princess And The Pea

Once upon a time there lived a handsome prince named Henry. Henry lived with his mother Alice, who was getting old. She would leave Henry the throne, only if he married a princess, so they arranged to meet some.

One day one hundred beautiful princesses came. Ninety-nine of them the prince didn't like.

'I'm sorry, it's princesses only,' said Alice to the girl left, however Henry seemed to like her. They all sat down to lunch.

'What is your name?' asked the prince.

'My name is Amelia.'

Alice thought, *she's not a princess; I'll set her a test to show me whether she's good enough for my son.*

The test began immediately and it started with manners - 10. cooking skills - 10. What she wants for her future - 10.

Alice had one more test for her and so she said, 'Will you sleep here tonight?'

'Okay.'

Alice ordered her butler to place a pea in the middle of the mattress and put five more mattresses on top of that.

It was time to go to bed and Alice said, 'They're for guests and as we only have you, you will have to sleep on them.'

'Okay.'

'Goodnight, darling,' squeaked the prince.

In the morning Amelia went downstairs for breakfast.

'Did you sleep well?'

'No, something was itching my back all night.'

At that point the queen let her into the family.

The reason Amelia felt the pea is because princesses have soft skin.

Sophie Tomkins (12)
Mayville High School, Southsea

Evil's Bane

Once, when the world was one continent, there existed a race of people divided. Many lived in the great kingdom of Tirowen, thieves lived in the desert and the peaceful folk lived in the forest. Which brings us to the hero. A young boy of around twelve with golden hair lay shivering in bed on a cold night. He woke suddenly, his eyes were blue and troubled, he wore a dark green tunic and had a sword strapped around his back. He was scruffy with a strange jewelled locket around his neck. His name was Gwyn, the greatest warrior in the forest.

'I must go Tirowen, there is great evil there.' With that he bounded out of bed and his home and left the forest. There he laid his eyes on the Field of Tor. He ran to the kingdom to discover he was too late and the once great city was in shreds.

A small glint caught Gwyn's eye, it was a small golden ball. He decided to take it with him. He tried to storm the castle but the path was destroyed. He turned, ready to leave, when he saw some strange markings on the wall. At the same time he felt heat in his pocket. He took the golden ball out but it had changed into a small instrument. When Gwyn played it a sword was revealed which transported him to evil Count Drallig.

There was a raging battle ending in Gwyn throwing the Evil's Bane to hit Drallig right in the head which killed him. Gwyn returned to the forest as protector of the kingdom.

Rhys Owen (12)
Mayville High School, Southsea

The Surfer

You struggle desperately with your wetsuit, force your boots on and cram your hands inside your gloves. Grabbing your board, stowing it under your arm and tearing furiously across the damp sand to where the waves softly break. You gasp as your toes hit the water, but forget the numbing cold and charge headlong into the surf.

Skimming your board in front of you, you dive onto it, paddling towards the horizon, before bracing yourself as a rogue wave engulfs you. You break through to sunlight and your jaw drops as a colossal, dark shadow rises out of the water and thunders towards you. Terrified and overjoyed you turn around, paddling feverishly to catch this water leviathan. With a swooping feeling in your stomach, you feel yourself hurtling forwards as the wave sweeps you along. With all the strength you can muster you push against the board with your hands, arch your back, bringing your lead leg forwards before gingerly standing up. You gain your balance whilst roaring an animal-like whoop of elation as you soar down an infinite slope of living water, all the while chased by a swirling, crashing, splashing tunnel of light and everything in the world suddenly makes sense; this is surely the reason that the universe was created, for this single instant of sheer ecstasy?

The other surfers hear and understand - as does the wave as it surges on in a swirling maelstrom of boiling foam, while you collapse into the cool, calm, soothing water.

Matthew Williams (15)
Milton Abbey School, Blandford Forum

All Is Empty And Dark

Lost in my own troubled mind I stumble to the peak, the world has no meaning without that which I so desperately seek in this barren place. My thoughts tremble on the edge, my mind swirls back and forth agonisingly fast and with it my body rocks teetering towards finality.

With one small step I plummet towards her, I feel her getting closer drawn by an inexplicable force. Her spirit is all around me now, and I can feel the warmth of her skin against mine. I can feel her breath against my neck and I can almost see her beautiful form just out of the reach of perception. I continue taking in all the different sensations and feelings and emotions that flood my head. I can sense something in me that I haven't felt for an age, something fills the empty void of eternal longing in my heart. I feel as though she falls alongside me in the place she never wanted me to go. Then like a candle blown out by icy winds, there is nothing, just oblivion and the same longing deep in my chest.

Something rouses me and I try to cling on to things for a long time, to memorise the textures, to absorb her spirit into mine. I reflect on how all things end. Love, life, happiness, it is all a twilight dance that we intertwine in, spirits mix, laughter rises and falls, and in the end it is all still a witching hour dream that spins away into oblivion as the sun rises and our lives fade out.

Nick Turner (17)
Milton Abbey School, Blandford Forum

I'm Not Mad

I wake up and I'm terrified. I think I've been terrified before. Maybe it was the same the last time I woke up. Maybe not. My emotions drift above my head while I look at them through cold eyes. I can't remember anything. In my mind I can feel memories twisting away from me faster than I can catch them. Sometimes people tell me I'm mad, but I'm not mad as long as there's a reason for everything I do. I can remember that. If I can't find a reason to be terrified then that means I've gone mad and I won't let myself go mad.

I look around. White floor, white walls, white ceiling. A white door as well. Have I ever seen what's on the other side? I get off the bed and the floor is soft. I lose my balance and try to steady myself on the wall, but my arms are trapped across my chest in a white coat. White coat. Trapped. Helpless. My breath catches in my throat as the terror finally descends on me and logical thought is buried. I struggle against leather straps as fear pulls my legs out from under me and I fall to the floor. The door opens and rough hands grab my arms, lifting me onto the bed. Pain in my arm and the world starts to fade away. I stop struggling, but I still know one thing. I had a reason to be terrified and I'm not mad.

Alexander Shepherd (16)
Milton Abbey School, Blandford Forum

The Black Tides

It was just a normal day for Mr Flint Westwood or so he thought. He was driving back from his job when a suspicious-looking man was walking down the side of the road. The man was wearing a long overcoat, quite large boots and walked with a limp and he was quite a slow walker. Flint watched him for a bit, but a large lorry passed in front of him and he lost sight of the man, he thought he had gone into the alley and thought nothing of it.

As he carried on driving down the road he thought he saw the same man, a strong case of a flashback, that sight still lingered in his head.

When he parked his car, he walked into the house and sat down and watched TV for a couple of hours. As he channel flicked, he ended up on the news which he found quite interesting. It was said that a virus had escaped and was literally turning people into zombies. As he looked intensely at the screen he noticed that one of the 'things' looked exactly like the man he had seen on the street.

Suddenly a big bang on the glass door. Flint went to the curtains, pulled them and jumped back, for there was one of the most grotesque things at the window he'd ever seen. He closed them quickly and moved back. He jumped again because the phone rang. It was the police chief, he said they had a situation and they needed Flint's help …

Thomas Poate (15)
Milton Abbey School, Blandford Forum

The Blade In The Night

The grapple gave a dull clunk. The dark figure sighed, checked the grapple was secure with a swift tug. The night was a dark one, picked because no moon shone, a perfect night for dark deeds. With expert skill, born into him through dark blood, the figure climbed the wall in one fluid motion, landing on two feet on the battlement walkway. He stared up, above him loomed the vast mass which was the outline of the massive castle of Shogun Lord Tami Kade. A lone guard passed towards the figure in black. As he passed the guard gasped and fell spluttering. The figure removed the garotter from the now silent guard's neck. He would have to be quick, any more instances like this and he would be passing into the other world as well.

He took aim and began to spin the grapple and rope in a fast rotation and it flew silently across the main courtyard and caught on the top rafter above the topmost window sill. He waited for a few moments and when no sound was made he smiled to himself, *the guards are dozy tonight*. Again, in a flash, the figure swung across the courtyard and landed effortlessly and silently on the dark window ledge.

In front of him stretched a sea of smooth timber floor and in the centre his objective, a large bed of many hangings that housed his lordship. The figure crept towards the bed, he stiffened. To his right and left he heard muffled sounds. He calculated what the sounds were; guards moving in near sleep in secret compartments in the wall. With no sound he walked to the bed, pulled back the hangings. The last thing the lord saw as he woke was the flash of a sword.

James Whitlock (15)
Milton Abbey School, Blandford Forum

Almost A Tale Of Two Birds Glued To A Lamp Post

An old paper bag floated up into the air. It playfully ducked and dived following the contours of the land, teasing but never quite touching. It was reflected in glistening puddles and bounced along in the wind. Finally it took rest against a rusting lamp post.

The sun's rays gracefully rose from the bag and crept up the aged post. They stumbled upon two fed-up and bedraggled-looking birds. One answered to the name of Trev and the other Bob.

Bob turned to face Trev and said, 'Looks like it's going to be a nice day Trev.'

'You're not wrong,' replied Bob.

These birds spoke in an Australian accent and were in fact glued to the top of the lamp post.

'I can't believe we're still stuck to this post Bob.'

'I know what you mean Trev. I've seen four people that I don't like the look of, and I haven't been able to defecate on a single one. It drives me to despair.'

It was the beginning of the third day of the pair's misadventure on the post and the novelty had started to wear a bit thin.

'I mean seriously Bob, who in this day and age glues a bird to a lamp post?'

'You're telling me Trev. What did he think he was playing at?'

With that the pair put in a fantastic effort, after flapping frantically they took off and disappeared into the clear morning sky.

Samuel Gell (18)
Milton Abbey School, Blandford Forum

The Thing

There it was again! I'm sure it was it, that thing! It was poking out at me, staring. My heart pounded as I grasped my bag completely motionless! I wasn't sure what I could possibly do. As I reached for my weapon of choice, it moved and I jumped so high up in the air that my head was nearing the ceiling. Once I had recovered myself, slowly but surely I moved the bag that was grasped in the moment away from the spot where it had vanished. Clasping my weapon of choice, which at that point was a shoe, with one hand and moving the bag with the other, I peered down beyond the bag with eagle eyes, ready to snap at anything that moved.

The bag had been moved and as my eyes adjusted to the harsh darkness, I had my shoe at the ready. It was scary, my arm was shaking but I knew that I should keep on going. As my eyes focused on the small area of round that I was concentrating on, something caught my eye. Was it the thing I asked myself? I turned my head slower than a snail moves and eventually was level with my opponent. Unknowingly my hand came rushing down as if an unknown force had grasped it onto my opponent. The shoe, which I was holding, squashed it, leaving a nasty stain on the ground. I had ended it. Now I could return to bed.

Tom Barrow (15)
Milton Abbey School, Blandford Forum

The Hambro Head Of House

Back in September 2005AD Marcus Maximuss was made Hambro head of house. He was the worst and most fierce head of house for hundreds of years. We were all used to the head of house not caring what our caves looked like or if we had a bit of fun in the house. But this was no more. Now caves had to be immaculate and if anyone was found having fun they would be punished severely by the dreaded dead arm or even worse, being reported to the housemaster.

I remember there was a young lad, his name was George Oreileus, a very brave and handsome young man, went on leaving his cave in a mess or messing around after bedtime. Marcus Maximuss was not pleased and confronted George, but was sent away with a witty comment or was ignored altogether even though Marcus was a beast of a man.

After a few months of this Marcus was getting very angry and dragged the poor boy away by himself to a dark cave. He then proceeded to use his deafening scream and he was said to have threatened to dispose of the boy if he did not put an end to being so cheeky and the rest we cannot talk about, for the fear it would strike into the hearts of those who heard it. From then on George Oreileus was never the same witty young man he once was.

George Le Gallais (15)
Milton Abbey School, Blandford Forum

The Market

They never look dead, just asleep. This is an image I have of the fish at the market, especially the lobsters, glistening like knights in shining armour. You keep waiting for them to snap at you or for the salmon to flounder off the gutting board.

Going to the market with my mum was never a chore for me, more an experience, a bombardment on my young senses. The sounds of the portly, streetwise sellers calling out their latest bargains like flower-attracting insects, with its smell and bright colours in an attempt to lure business.

And the smells, they attack you all at once, enveloping you in their pungent grasp. There is the cheese stall, with all its disgusting odours leaking across the street and the tendency to follow you around like an over-zealous dog, long after you have left the vicinity.

The attack does not stop there however, the tempting sights of the large, voluptuous cherries, ripe to bursting, and the apples, so many different kinds, turning choosing fruit into a hunt for the largest, firmest fruit the stall has to offer.

The myriad collection of all manner of people also draws your attention; the toothless old man who seems to sell the same toys and never do any business, but seems perfectly content amongst the market mayhem. Or the rather glum-looking youth, shackled to the greeting card stall with a look of utter boredom on his face until someone pulls out a banknote. The market.

Nicolas Rainey (15)
Milton Abbey School, Blandford Forum

A Day In The Life Of A Bird

A bird can go anywhere it wants, whenever it wants. It is free to go anywhere it wishes because there are no boundaries when you are up there in the sky. No roads or traffic lights to stop you. No one to tell you where not to go. There are no borders to cross or anything like that. You can sleep wherever you like, like you are a traveller. Whenever you feel hungry you can just swoop down to human level and scavenge for food off people like a hyena.

You can look down and laugh at the humans in their cars that are stuck in a traffic jam while there is nothing in front of you but open air for miles and miles.

You can travel to any country or place in the whole world for free while humans have to pay to fly. Flying around is quicker and easier than walking or swimming. A nest is very comfortable and cosy and can be built anywhere from the side of a vertical cliff to a branch on a small tree. Birds can reach places that a human could never dream of getting to without expensive equipment.

Richard Hagenbuch (15)
Milton Abbey School, Blandford Forum

The Monster Of Loch Ness

The monster of Loch Ness had supposedly killed Adrian's old father when he was out fishing on the loch, they only found splintered remains of his boat. Adrian wanted to find out.

It was a misty morning when Adrian was eating breakfast. He could not see the huge hill that loomed over the cottage for the mist. There was a tapping on the door. Adrian wiped milk off his beard, he was looked down upon by three beaming faces at the door. They were expert marine biologists, Mark, Scott and William.

As they drove along the winding roads lugging the heavy kit, the three explained that they were also interested in the beast. They had worked out that it could be some type of ancient dragon.

'I just want to kill it,' said Adrian.

The biologists thoroughly disagreed. They then walked to a small fishing boat and piled the kit in.

Once on the loch Mark and Scott set up the radar system while William put on an extremely heavy diving suit. Then Adrian poured blood into the loch. The three others lowered William into the loch shallows, he walked right in. But then a large object appeared on the radar screen.

'My God!' Adrian, Mark and Scott said in unison.

But it was too late. The rope and William's air tube whipped away violently and snapped the rudder it was attached to. A huge mass of air rushed to the surface. Adrian dived in, the other two protested. Suddenly a huge, smooth back appeared on the surface. The shore was not far away, Adrian swam for it, the back followed him slowly. Then a huge head towered above him, it had a set of huge, slanted, backward teeth and a tiny pair of small black eyes. Adrian froze. But the head turned back to the boat.

The huge eel-like monster crushed the boat with its huge slimy body and rudder-like tail. It took Mark in its jaws and crushed him till blood came out of his mouth. The monster must have been thirty foot long and five foot thick.

Nothing was seen of Scott and that was the last sighting of the Loch Ness monster.

Hugo Mann (15)
Milton Abbey School, Blandford Forum

The Wild, Wild West

Texas, Arkansas, in the time of the cowboys. Big Gun Bill was walking through the eastern side of New Mine Milton, heading for the town square. In the centre of New Mine Milton, the infamous Slick Hips Jim was testing his reactions. He drew and shot from the hip pointing across the square with his Smith and Wesson 8-shot revolvers.

The tension was running high and the blood running thin. Big Gun Bill rocked up, spurs clinking in the fresh silence as the two stared at each other in the midday heat. The stereotypical tumbleweed flew past, testing the ground like a swallow over a lake. The two's hands became poised over their holsters and then … as if in slow motion, the pistols were drawn almost simultaneously. The noise of hard steel against the worn leather and then a sharp, ear-piercing bang. Then silence coated the town once again.

The peace was broken with a heavy thud of Big Gun Bill hitting the floor, the sand flew up around his carcass. The warm blood trickled from the cavity in his chest, saturating the dust surrounding it. Big Gun Bill's side-kick and fellow eastsiders ran to his side, but it was too late. Slick Hips turned and proceeded to walk without seeming to break into a sweat, cool as an ice cube. He headed off into the distance leaving the fatal disruption behind him.

Michael Gell (15)
Milton Abbey School, Blandford Forum

The Deranged Leprechaun

Over one hundred years ago in Ireland, there lived a leprechaun. When you see a leprechaun, he gives you three wishes, but not this one ... No, this one gave you three lashes. The one thing he kept close to his heart was his gold.

One day his gold was taken by the town farmer, so when the leprechaun came back, he went to look for it, but it was not there. He was so mad. He took out his gun, his bow and arrow, and his flame torch, and went to find his good mate, Mr Unicorn.

When he told the unicorn, he was pretty mad too. So he fetched his weapons and they went to find the farmer. When they got there they saw the gold. The leprechaun then got out his bow and arrow, set it alight and shot the farmer.

When the leprechaun saw the farmer's wife, he fell in love. So, he took her and the gold, let the unicorn eat the animals, and lived happily ever after!

Nathan Barry (14)
Moyles Court School, Ringwood

Space Invaders

Long ago in a galaxy far away there was a space landing port. Next to it was a control base. It looked small on the outside but inside it was massive. The leader of the control base was Captain Panaka. The captain was blue-skinned with short red highlighted hair. He had had yet another bad sleep after waking up twice during the night.

That night the Mars United Vs AC Pluto football match was played and everybody on board was watching the match on Space Sports. It was half-time and suddenly alarms started to go off and everyone rushed to his room. The computers had gone fuzzy red and then crashed.

'Sproket, call the jupitorian to have a look,' shouted the captain.

In the morning everything went quiet including the computers. Captain Panaka was worried, 'Why has everything gone quiet?'

'There was a message from Alpha moon base. They said that there was a giant space bird on the loose with two other aliens with him.'

'Get to your ships. We've got a mission to solve.'

Meanwhile Captain Panaka and his assistant, Sproket, were making a plan, a plan to capture the space bird. In their plan they decided to shoot it with a plasma rocket.

Straight away Sproket went to his ship to load up his plasma rockets. 'I will do it on my own,' said Sproket.

Minutes later they all saw a flash of orange and a star shoot through the air. After, they all cheered three times and went back to watch the second leg of the knockout cup of Space Sports.

Danny Whitelock (12)
Moyles Court School, Ringwood

Marlit Attacks

I was running for my life. The thing I was running from was weird; it was a robot on the outside but a gory substance on the inside with two eyes and a hole for a mouth. If you touched it you would burn to death.

I thought I'd lost it; then I saw out of the corner of my eye, a car, so I quickly smashed the window and jumped in. I turned the key, the car revved, I looked behind me and saw a shadow, it found me so I slammed the accelerator and the car shot forward, I was safe.

When I got home I contacted MI6 because I worked there. My name was Ollie, I was a special agent and I was twenty-five years old. I drove down there and explained what had happened. As soon as I told them what it looked like, they showed me a file on it. Its name was Marlit and it had fallen to Earth two days earlier.

Four days later I picked up the newspaper and it had a picture of Marlit and a dead man next to it. The picture was taken in Ringwood, so I got dressed and went down there. When I got there I called for a back-up team to search the area …

Oliver Hayter (12)
Moyles Court School, Ringwood

A Story Of A Baked Bean Can

It was a nice sunny day at can school, when suddenly two policecans came into the grounds. Without looking at anyone, they walked straight into the building.

After break we all went to the science room. We were doing about: What's inside our cans? Then out of the blue Miss P, the headmistress came into our classroom. She looked upset. She called me into her office. 'Benny, I have some bad news. Your parents are dead.'

I was distraught, I didn't know what to do or think. That led me to the question of, who did it and why? I quit school and started asking around. First I went to Peter the pea can. Peter was an old family friend. I had heard stories about him but had never seen him, until now. He said I should look near the bin. I did as he said, but when I got there all I saw was Peter. He was holding up a sign saying, *I Killed Your Parents*. I quickly ran at him. When I got there we started to wrestle. We were wrestling for at least five minutes. Then, with one big shove, I pushed him off the edge.

This is how I came to be here ... in jail.

Dalton North (13)
Moyles Court School, Ringwood

A Day In The Life Of My Dog

I woke up confused. Why was I in my dog's basket?

I looked down and saw black and white fur. I started to scream but it just came out as a bark. Was I dreaming? How did it happen? I was my dog!

Mum called, 'Freddy, it's time for a walk.'

Would she know it was me? She didn't notice as she put on my collar. I had never felt so excited before a walk.

As I was let off my lead I felt so full of energy. No wonder the real Freddy was always so lively. I jumped up on Mum and muddy paws went everywhere. Then I smelt something. It was rabbit. I ran as fast as I could. I lost the trail but was also lost in a huge wood.

I charged around listening for a call but it was silent. I ran in what I thought was the direction of home. Was I right? Yes! There was Mum looking as worried as ever.

When we got home I played in the garden but then I heard a tub open. My food was coming. I tucked into it but couldn't believe I was eating dog food. I needed a sleep after all that running and settled down on the sofa. It was nice being a dog.

When I woke up, I heard someone yell, 'Samantha, get off, you're filthy.' It was back to normal. Freddy was clean. Did he know we had swapped lives? It will always be our secret.

Samantha Buck (12)
Moyles Court School, Ringwood

Tiger Girl

Mary was obsessed with tigers. She had always dreamed of talking to tigers. One day Mary saw a mystical shop. There was a sign saying, 'For £5, talk to any animal you like'. Mary was so excited. She ran into the store, but nobody was there so she rang the bell on the desk.

'Hello!' said the shopkeeper, as he bolted up from behind his desk.

Mary screamed in shock.

'I'm sorry for scaring you. How can I help?'

'I would like to talk to tigers.'

The shopkeeper picked up a black bottle. 'Drink this before you go to bed.'

When she woke up, she got out of bed and went downstairs.

Her mother screamed, 'Tiger!' and ran away.

Mary looked in the mirror and roared, 'I'm a tiger!' She went upstairs to read the bottle, which said, 'This potion is to turn people into tigers. Use carefully'.

Mary sprinted to the shop. Everywhere people were screaming, 'Tiger', but she kept going.

'You have to reverse it!' she shouted at the shopkeeper. He snapped his fingers and she woke up in a hospital bed. 'Where am I?' she asked drowsily.

'Oh darling, you're awake!' Mary's mother screamed with joy. 'You got hit. You have been in a coma, and we thought we had lost you.' Her eyes filled with joyful tears.

'Don't worry, I'll be OK,' Mary reassured her.

The whole family were glad she was OK. Mary was still obsessed with tigers, but she would never let it go too far!

Shaunie Huzzey (12)
Moyles Court School, Ringwood

The Giant Jelly Baby

Susan and Stuart were fighting and knocked some jelly babies into the sink that was filled with water.

'Stop fighting and go to bed!' yelled their mother.

They ran out of the kitchen and into their rooms but Stuart grabbed the rest of the jelly babies, leaving the other ones inside the sink.

The house was quiet. Everyone was asleep. Suddenly a jelly baby jumped out of the sink. He was green, wet and was wearing a red belt. He wandered into Susan's room. The jelly baby grabbed a strawberry lace attached it to his belt and looped it round a glass on Susan's desk. He climbed up the rope but struggling, he fell onto Susan's pillow, where he lay down and fell asleep.

The next morning she was walking to school, when she thought, *oh no! The bullies.* She started walking faster, when the school bullies stepped in front of her.

Suddenly there was a flash and the green thing grew and grew until it was six feet tall. It was a giant jelly baby. He grabbed the bullies and lifted them into the air warning them not to scare anyone again. The bullies ran off. Susan stood still in shock at what she had seen.

There was another flash and the jelly baby turned back to its normal size. Then out of nowhere an army of coloured jelly babies appeared and carried the green jelly baby away.

Sarah Dickinson (13)
Moyles Court School, Ringwood

The Possessed Portrait

The plaque upon the painting read: *Lady Caroline of Schutenberg, 1941.* I looked up at the woman in the portrait just as she smiled and winked at me. Following this, a protruding hand wandered out and grabbed my dress by the collar and tugged. Suddenly there was a buzzing and electric yellow lines entwined themselves into perfect circles around my head. I screamed. However nothing came out.

A few seconds later, I landed hard on the floorboards next to Lady Caroline. She pulled me up and without speaking a word, handed me a beautiful hand-made box.

I looked at her with a bewildered expression and with that she started to explain herself.

'I want you to do me a favour,' she started. 'Could you possibly hide this for me?'

'Sure. Why?' I asked in a confused tone of voice.

'Because those insolent Germans are going to come within a few days and I'm sure they will take what's precious to me,' she said under her breath. 'So will you take it?'

'Of course I will,' I said, eager to take a glance at the old box.

'Thank you,' she said, clapping her hands. She gave me a great shove and I felt myself falling, falling out of the painting and landing on the museum's floor with a thump.

After heaving myself up, I surveyed the box closely. Then I opened it, the electric yellow circles came back. *Oh no!* I thought as I swayed into darkness …

Bethany Hume (12)
Moyles Court School, Ringwood

The Life Of A Clownfish

My eyes open as the sun lights my eyes and my fins sway in the currents as the water pushes by. I swim in and out of my anemone, which is my home. It helps scare predators away. My eyes are wide open in search of any food which comes my way. My main meal is brine shrimp, as it's the easiest food to catch. I swallow it whole in just one big gulp.

I live with my partner, whose colour is bright orange with white stripes. We swim together everywhere and we look out for each other, watching each other's backs. When we have time on our hands, we like to play in our anemone, chasing each other round and round, but sometimes we just lie on our sides and sleep for hours on end. When the day is over, we catch our last meal. As the sun sets, we snuggle up in the anemone's tentacles and sleep till the start of a new day.

Cameron Leverell Oag (13)
Moyles Court School, Ringwood

Shopping Centre Blast

A disturbing incident took place in the early hours of this morning. There was an explosion on the outskirts of London at Bluewater. An estimated ten thousand people were inside the shopping centre. The fire crew have been trying to tackle the blaze for five hours. It was suspected that it began with an explosion in the lower parts of the building, where thousands of gas canisters were stored.

At this point in time, investigators are looking into the cause of the blast. It is not certain how many people were trapped in the fire, but it is thought to be in excess of three thousand. It will be a massive task to trace all the missing persons. Ten bodies have been recovered so far, but the death toll is expected to rise dramatically.

I spoke to John Ball, who was caught up in the blaze. He said, 'I can't believe I am still alive. My family and I were just about to go into W H Smith, when, all of a sudden, there was a roar as the ground shook. There was absolute chaos as everyone ran screaming and pushing. Thank goodness we got out safely, but some people obviously weren't as fortunate'.

We can only wait to see what the investigation uncovers over the coming days, as Bluewater comes to terms with its biggest disaster in modern times.

Alexander Haigh (12)
Moyles Court School, Ringwood

Pont Audemer Vs Ringwood

Ringwood table tennis, who were hoping for a hat-trick, had a good game against Pont Audemer, tennis de table. The French having the number sixty-three in France, and a very strong order, looked certain for victory.

After the morning groups, the match was still uncallable. With four Ringwood players top in their group, and three second, Pont Audemer got the rest.

With there being thirty-one players in the morning, and Pont Audemer's number one arriving late in the first round, number one played thirty-one and so on. The player with the 'bye' was Ringwood, number six (Matt Haynes)

He then, in the second round, had to play the Pont Audemer number one (Laurent). The first game was close, with Laurent winning it 11-8. Laurent then struggled as Matt showed his potential. Laurent won that game 11-9. In the third Matt's head went down as Laurent tried to show off, but lost that game 7-11. After winning the third he looked like he would win the fourth, when he was 9-5 up, but the Pont Audemer player fought back and won the game 12-10. The score was 8, 9-7, 10. This game was described as the best game all day.

When the day had finished the Ringwood players claimed they had been cheated, because the Pont Audemer player who came second, lost three, and Ringwood player who came nineteenth lost one.

All in all it was a very good day. Pont Audemer won, this year.

Matthew Haynes (14)
Moyles Court School, Ringwood

The Ghost Of The Moyles Court Boarding House

On a cold and crisp night, Jenny, Kirsty and Michelle were up telling ghost stories, when a shadow appeared at the door. Then suddenly Nathan jumped into the room.

'Run!' shouted Nathan.
'What is it?' cried Jenny.
'He's here,' replied Nathan. 'Run!'
They all ran out and down the hall to the caféteria.
'He's coming,' wailed Michelle.
As they reached the door Jenny cried out, 'It's locked.'
'Oh no,' squealed Kirsty.

Nathan shouted at them to move and he ran at the door and it crashed open. Then all four jumped over the counters like rabbits.

'Shh.' whispered Nathan. 'It's OK everythin ...'

Then there was a loud bang, the man threw a rake down on a counter. The look of the leaves and dripping water made them feel even more scared than they were.

'I think he's leaving,' whispered Kirsty. 'Come on!'
'Wait, out the window,' interrupted Nathan.

They slithered over to the window and climbed up and over and out the other side.

The rain was heavy and cold on their feet. They were about to head back over to the boarding house when they saw him in the distance with his rake at his side.

'What do we do?' screamed Michelle. 'What do we do?'

'Wait,' said Nathan. He walked over to the man, he had his head down. 'Reg ... ?'

Oliver Unt (14)
Moyles Court School, Ringwood

Boy Gets Jumped By Classroom Bullies

Daniel Smith of Hampshire ended up in casualty last night with a fractured skull and four broken ribs after being jumped from behind by three bullies from his school. All three of them took him down and then repeatedly kicked him in the head and ribs. They then ran off after a couple of minutes and left him hanging by his shirt collar on the school back gate railings.

He was found by an elderly lady and was flown by helicopter to Salisbury district hospital, where the A & E trauma team awaited his arrival. He is now in intensive care, after having undergone brain surgery late last night. The doctors say he is now stable and recovering well.

Daniel's mother, Anita Smith, spoke to us and said, 'We are so grateful to the doctors and nurses here at the hospital. Without them, Daniel might not even be alive. We would also like to thank the Salisbury Police Department for doing such a great job of tracking down and catching the three brutes who did this to our Daniel'.

Previously we had also spoken to Sergeant D Henderson about the prosecution of the three boys who attacked Daniel, he said, 'When we spoke to one boy, at first he was scared and dazed but after some time we were able to get the information we needed from him and have since found the three culprits and they are currently awaiting prosecution'.

Gemma Fraser (13)
Moyles Court School, Ringwood

Monty's Terror

Last week Mrs Cath Banks and her little Jack Russell terrier called Monty, were walking in a nearby park, where Monty was attacked.

'It was a sunny afternoon. I was walking Monty as usual,' Cath said. 'Suddenly these two massive Alsatians ran up to me'.

One of the Alsatians jumped up at Cath. She fell to the ground. Luckily she was not injured. The other Alsatian went for Monty. Cath scrambled to her feet. She was horrified to see Monty in the Alsatian's mouth. Cath tried to grab hold of Monty. 'I didn't know what to do. My heart was racing,' says Cath.

After a long struggle Cath held Monty in her arms. Monty's back was badly bleeding.

Cath looked around for the owner of the Alsatians. A man walked over to her. 'He had a smile on his face,' Cath recalls. 'I could not believe he was not helping'.

The owner said, 'Sorry about that,' and he left.

Cath rushed Monty to the vet. He had a life-threatening operation which left him with a permanent scar.

Mali Griffiths (13)
Moyles Court School, Ringwood

Back Garden Mystery

It was June 27th 1974 and it was glorious day. However, the heat and the sun couldn't stop it turning out to be the most fatal day at Merryfield Junior.

At break the children were playing kick ball. Mo, the best kick ball player Merryfield had ever seen, was in good form. However his good kicking ability fatally ended his life.

It was Mo's turn to kick. The ball got thrown and Mo kicked it so high, they couldn't see it in the sunlight. Suddenly a fielder shouted, 'There it is.'

All the children watched as it flew into the garden at the back of the playground. The playground went quiet. Everyone had heard about a young boy who once went in the garden to get a ball and never returned.

I'm going over!' said Mo in a determined voice as he strutted up to the fence.

All the children saluted him and there were calls like, 'There's one brave kid walking over there', and 'Mo please come back alive'.

Mo placed his foot on the side and pulled himself over the fence. He gave one last look back and then jumped down. The ball was thrown over and the playground erupted with cheers. Then everyone realised Mo hadn't returned. All the children ran up to look over the fence. All that was left was Mo's baseball cap and wristband. Mo was never seen again but lived in the memory as the best kick ball player ever seen at Merryfield Junior.

Ryan Saunders (13)
Moyles Court School, Ringwood

Mysterious House

It was a Friday night and Paul was sleeping over Nick's house. 'What shall we do?' he said.

'How about going for a walk in the forest? There's an abandoned house,' said Nick.

'Let's go.'

They walked through the dark forest with the trees hanging over them. In the distance they could see the house. As they were drawn closer to the house, they could see a figure by the smashed window. They slowly walked towards the doorstep. The door screeched open. They stumbled up the old creaky stairs to find blood on the floor and a dusty knife on a bench. They turned on a torch and went into another room to find nothing of interest.

They went back to the other room to find that the knife had gone. They could see a shadow. It was someone holding a knife up towards them. They ran down the stairs and outside. The both split up and went down separate paths. The shadow was chasing Paul but could not catch him. It slashed the letter E onto his T-shirt. He managed to jump a fence and get away.

'That was close wasn't it Paul!'

'Yeah!'

'Let's come back tomorrow.'

They came back the next day to find that he wasn't there and building work had started. The house was going to be called 'Empire Estate'.

Paul and Nick never told a soul about it.

Edward Hodgson-Egan (13)
Moyles Court School, Ringwood

The Robbery

On Tuesday 24th October the jewellery shop 'Diamonds for Everyone' was broken into. The three men who did this were dressed in black and had guns. They shot at the windows and the glass shattered into tiny pieces and fell to the ground. When the men eventually left they were able to clear up the glass. They then looked to see what they had stolen. It looked as if they had nothing. No one could find what was missing. They looked on all the shelves but there was not a gap anywhere. The police came to the conclusion that they did not find what they were looking for.

Four days later a top celebrity came into the shop looking for a ring for her wedding. She was so excited and loved the wide variety they had. She eventually chose a few she wanted to try.

She tried one on and it looked amazing. She said, 'This is the one. I have to have it'. She then took it off and noticed a gold mark around her finger. She pointed it out to the staff member and he went to get the manager.

The manager came back not looking very pleased. He picked up the ring and said, 'I think we have found what those men broke into our shop for. To swap expensive jewellery for their fake stuff'.

The celebrity looked devastated.

The manager then said, 'Don't worry. We will find the real ones'.

Kirsty Osborne (14)
Moyles Court School, Ringwood

Beware Of The Woods!

It is an average morning at Moyles Court School. The clock reaches half-past ten. All the children run out to the paddock. It has deep, dense woods behind it. These wood are mysterious - too mysterious for a child's mind.

There were three best friends, Tom, George and Ryan who thought they were soldiers. They went deeper and deeper into the forest. Then they came across the giant white structure which was hanging between two old trees.

Tom said, 'That's weird to build a climbing frame in the middle of the forest.'

Ryan added in a sarcastic tone of voice, 'That's one of Mr Dean's brilliant ideas!'

The three boys started to climb. They soon started to find the frame becoming sticky. They heard a hissing noise from above their heads. Tom suddenly got drenched. It was not rain, it was saliva, coming from the gaping mouth of the gigantic spider above their heads. Ryan and George managed to wriggle away and break free. When their feet hit the ground, they picked up some branches from the forest floor. They repeatedly hit the spider again and again, more violently with each swing.

Tom managed to release himself from the spider's grasp. Ryan was gazing behind the others. Then Tom and George looked. There were millions of eggs covering the forest floor. These eggs were hatching.

They ran with great haste . . .

George Soan (13)
Moyles Court School, Ringwood

The Final Battle

King Arthur was married to Queen Guinevere. They lived in Camelot. Guinevere and Lancelot were lovers. The Knights of the Round Table found Guinevere guilty of treason, she was sentenced to death! The queen was ready to die, Lancelot rescued her and took her to live in his castle in France.

King Arthur took his army to fight Lancelot and to kill Guinevere. He needed 3,000 soldiers and 100 lions, so he asked Merlin for help.

When they got to France they went straight to the castle. Lancelot had his men ready, he had 800 men to fight. They let the lions go and Arthur and all his soldiers ran towards Lancelot's men. The lions ripped Lancelot's men up and his men chopped their heads off. Some of the lions got killed.

Merlin came back and brought his stick claw and he hid because he needed power to kill most of them. He got more power and killed more people. Merlin was upset. King Arthur told him not to worry.

A week later they found out that Lancelot was still alive. Arthur was not strong. Guinevere went back to King Arthur, so he could kill her.

Lancelot got some of his men together to save his queen.

Adam Leslie (14)
Philip Southcote School, Addlestone

The Final Battle

King Arthur was married to Queen Guinevere, they lived in Camelot. Guinevere and Lancelot were lovers. The Knights of the Round Table found Guinevere guilty of treason, she was sentenced to death. The Queen was ready to die when Lancelot rescued her and took her to live in his castle in France.

King Arthur took his army to fight Lancelot. He and his knights were getting ready for the battle with Lancelot. They were on their way to France and they came across a big snake so they got their swords out and Arthur cut the snake's head off and skinned it.

They carried on and they saw a river. They looked for a way across and found a big tree which they cut down and made a bridge with so they could cross the river.

They got to France and went to Lancelot's castle. Arthur said, 'We shall rest here.'

The next morning Lancelot woke up and Arthur was gone. He went down to the door and a messenger came to him and said Arthur had gone to fight Mordred. Lancelot went to help Arthur to fight Mordred in Camelot.

He got to Camelot and Arthur had already started to fight and Lancelot went in to help. The fight was over and Mordred was killed by Arthur and Lancelot. Arthur was still King of England, Lancelot married Guinevere and had ten children. Lancelot went back to live in France in his castle. Arthur stayed in Camelot.

John Hockley (14)
Philip Southcote School, Addlestone

The Squeaky Wedding

It was a lovely morning for a wedding. Inside the church the vicar was arranging the flowers when he heard a squeaking noise coming from his feet. He glanced down and saw a brown fur ball scuttling past him. Suddenly he realised it was a rat! He grabbed his coat and quickly ran to the town. When he got there, not one shop had any traps left.

The vicar had to go back to the church and think of another idea. He went to the fridge and grabbed a few slices of cheese that would work until the wedding was over. Soon people were starting to arrive and the wedding was just beginning.

The vicar was halfway through talking when he heard a squeak. The guests all looked at each other. He quickly carried on and everyone turned back around.

Just as the rats were about to squeak, the vicar coughed halfway through his sentence so no one would suspect anything.

He kept this up for a while longer, but the rats started to enter from behind the wall. People saw them and screamed frantically.

One jumped in the bride's mother's hat and started nibbling at the fruit. Another one ran up the groom's trousers and ripped them with its claws. The final rat lunged onto the bride's dress when she was running out and her dress gave way.

Everyone jumped into the cars and drove away as fast as they could. The vicar sat down with his head in his hands.

Sophie Jackson (13)
Staunton Park Community School, Havant

The Icy Forest

… As Stacy slipped on the frozen floor, a gust of icy-cold wind rushed through the trees throwing bitterly sharp ice in her face. The sharp pain of the ice felt as if a million pins were being prodded into her face all at once.

Stacy struggled to leap up, but she was attached to a bush of thorns that were ripping at her trousers like a pack of hungry dogs biting through her new jeans to reach her flesh. When she broke free, she found that her legs were all bloody.

Something, from the corner of Stacy's eye, rushed through the trees, swift as a fox.

Stacy started to run, as fear bounced around in her mind, it wasn't a fox she saw, it was a pack of *wolves!* All of a sudden she halted. There in front of her was a fast flowing river, crashing up the banks.

As she turned around to see if there was another way out, the wolves surrounded her. She was trapped …

Michaela George (12)
Staunton Park Community School, Havant

The Ghostly Graveyard

As I walked through the dark, gloomy graveyard of Appleton Town, a shiver ran down my spine. I took a short cut through the graveyard. I don't know why but it was like something was pulling me to it.

There was no life to the graveyard. It was like someone or something had sucked the life out of it. As I carried on walking, the mist started looming; drifting in and out of the gravestones. Suddenly something stopped me. I turned left and saw a huge gravestone. Engraved on it, in gold letters, was the name 'Betty Stuart'. I moved closer to the gravestone.

I know your name, I thought. *That's my nan.* As I reached the gravestone, a blazing light nearly blinded me. The light was like the sun exploding. Before I knew it, right before my eyes, was my nan. I couldn't believe it. No one knew how my nan died exactly. She then told me she'd died peacefully in her sleep. I felt better knowing that she wasn't in pain. Five minutes later, she disappeared.

Suddenly I sat bolt upright. The sun was shining through my window. It must have been a dream. It couldn't be. I opened my curtains and looked out of the window. A rush of sadness hit me, knowing that I didn't really see her. Suddenly I saw, in the clouds, the face of my nan.

Rebecca Jones (13)
Swanmore Middle School, Ryde

The Haunted Warehouse

It was a sunny Friday afternoon and Ellie was walking home from school with her best friend Michelle. Ellie had golden hair and blue eyes. Michelle had black hair with blue streaks in.

On the way home Michelle spotted an old warehouse, she showed Ellie and asked, 'Can we go explore tonight?'

Ellie replied, 'Yes.'

When they got to Squirrel Lane, they said goodbye and ran home.

When Ellie got home she went upstairs and changed into cropped jeans and a top. She tied her hair into a ponytail and applied her make-up. She took her phone off charge and left to call for Michelle. Ellie texted her mum to say where she was.

As they got nearer and nearer to the warehouse Ellie got scared. They entered and looked around. It was like you had entered your worst nightmare and there were chains hanging down.

Suddenly there was a bang and Michelle screamed, Ellie grabbed Michelle and ran out the door, they ran all the way home and vowed never to return to the warehouse ever again.

Nicolle Hodges (12)
Swanmore Middle School, Ryde

Hurricane Ana

One hot, sunny day in Grand Cayman two best friends called Vicki and Amy went to seven mile beach for the day. Vicki was tall and had chocolate-brown hair. Amy was short and had blonde hair.

When they were on the beach the white sand was sliding through their toes, the clear aqua sea was gently lapping the shore. Everyone was smiling and laughing. They went to the wooden shack to get their surfboards. They swam out trying to catch a wave. They were having fun when all of a sudden the sky went from blue to black, it started to get really windy so they swam back. They lay on the beach from exhaustion from trying to fight back angry waves crashing against their fragile bodies.

The weather was getting worse. The shutters on the shack were banging loudly. The palm trees were swaying to and fro. They could hear this screaming voice telling them to get off the beach as Hurricane Ana was heading towards them.

They started to sprint to get off the beach when two palm trees flew down in front of them and caught fire. The waves were humongous crashing onto the beach with such a force. Vicki and Amy managed to get in the rescue hut, they were so tired.

Five hours later, Hurricane Ana had moved on. Vicki and Amy went outside to find their precious island in ruins.

Jade Smith (13)
Swanmore Middle School, Ryde

Don't Steal

Bill was having a normal boring old day until his mum came home from shopping. She had bought him a new computer game, because of that, his day just got better. Bill ran to his computer and put in the game, suddenly the door bell rang. It was his best mate Fred. As soon as possible Bill told Fred he had a new computer game called 'The Pharaoh's Tomb of Doom'. Finally the two boys started playing the game.

They were on the computer for a good hour and they both really liked it but Fred couldn't afford the game and was really cross that he didn't have it. As Fred was just about to go home he took the computer game and stuck it in his bag.

The next morning Bill ran down the stairs to his computer but the game had gone. He searched all around the house but there was no sign of it. When Bill walked to school he felt really bad. When he got to school he immediately asked Fred whether he had seen his game but he shouted no.

Meanwhile Fred's mum was clearing up the house when she found a computer game in Fred's room. She knew that this was Bill's game because Bill's mum had rung her up about it. So she took the game straight round to Bill's house and apologised. But as soon as Bill found out Fred was no longer his best mate!

Max Sampson (13)
Swanmore Middle School, Ryde

Dreaded Castle

Many years ago there was a dreaded castle and no one dared venture into the depths of the dark woods to where the castle stood tall and deserted.

Inside the castle lay the deadliest beast that ever hit Earth. The creature was 10 feet tall and had teeth as sharp as razors. People from the village said they'd seen the beast's scruffy black fur with icy, sharp claws opening the curtains on the dirty, dark, damp castle.

Many people came to fight the beast and, apparently, deep in the depths of the castle lay a prince who had been put to sleep for a wrongful thing he had done to his father.

Thousands of years passed, but no one got past the dark horrors of the castle. Until one day in the middle of May, Jodie, a princess, decided to find out what lay in the dark, gloomy castle.

She climbed up to the very top of the castle when suddenly … the castle shook vigorously as a massive roar shook the entire castle and the damp, dusty floor began to crumble beneath her, and then she saw it! A dark scruffy figure towering over her. The figure opened its mouth revealing razor-sharp fangs.

Suddenly, the floor trembled causing it to open up. Jodie's feet slipped as the dark hole guzzled her up. Soon Jodie hit the bottom and found herself lying in a bed next to a prince.

Unfortunately he's dead and so is she …

Jessica Pegram (12)
Swanmore Middle School, Ryde

The Rain

Man Killed By Earthworms!

A man has been killed whilst gardening. 36-year-old Mick Lewis was corroded, then eaten by a large group of, what seemed to be, ordinary earthworms. A neighbour observed the last part of the event but couldn't do anything to save him.

A few of the worms have been taken to a science laboratory for tests. So far the scientists have discovered that the worms contain some sort of powerful corrosive acid in their stomachs that they use to corrode and loosen up their prey before they feed. It is thought that the worms acquired this acid from chemicals leaked from a nuclear power plant. Investigations have begun to find out if this is true. There may also be a queen worm deep underground and if she is destroyed then we may have a chance of eliminating them all. The worms have temporarily been called 'munchers'.

These worms are deadly and a warning is going out to everyone that if they see any of these worms, to run. These creatures, 'munchers' are multiplying and until they are defeated everyone is advised to be on their guard and to, if they see any, contact the science laboratory on 0800 105 799.

Joe Peduzzi (11)
Swanmore Middle School, Ryde

Robot Rampage!

On Sunday the 15th of May all hell was let loose in the town of Loomsville.

A mad scientist, Dr Ogodon, claims to have made this monstrosity. 'I feel that I am to blame for this horror, but I assure you it was not on purpose.

I was just finishing off pouring the liquid metal into the head of the robot. After that, it was time for my lunch break, just as I was about to tuck into my ham and pickle sandwich, I realised that I had left the lab door open so, (me being as hungry as I was), I took a few more bites of my sandwich and ran to the lab'. He looks around the room and begins to speak again, 'As I peered into the lab, it looked a complete pigsty, then it came to me, I looked around for the metal I'd used on the robot's head. My wife had accidentally mixed the metals up, this means that the robot is used for bad instead of good, and that is why he has wrecked half the town. Eventually the robot will give in and break down, until then you'll just have to be careful, I'm very sorry for all that has happened and hope you can all stay safe for this short amount of time. It will be around 5-7 days before the robot will give in'.

Make sure you are not alone whilst walking the streets, keep your children away and most of all keep safe ...

Ellie Brentnall (12)
Swanmore Middle School, Ryde

The Day A Bad Cat Went Good

Once upon a time in a haunted house lived two witches, a good, kind, helpful witch Phoebe and a cruel, evil, mischievous witch Paige.

One fine summer's day (which Paige hated) Phoebe went out to buy the perfect witch's companion, a jet-black cat. So Phoebe bought the cat, named it Magic and set off back to the house.

Paige on the other hand was busy searching for her spell book Shadow who was magical so he could fly and respond to his own name. Phoebe walked in with a basket with a towel wrapped beautifully around it when she suddenly got startled by the sound of her sister! *'Phoebe is that you?'* Paige shrieked at the top of her voice.

'Yes it is me!' Phoebe cried. 'I have a special surprise for you.'

'Oh goody come here then and help me find that blooming book,' Paige shouted.

So Phoebe walked in the room and stared at her sister who wore a horrid black dress with dust smeared all over it and a long pointy hat which curled over at the top. Then Paige looked at Phoebe with an evil glare.

Phoebe wore a long violet dress with diamonds and rubies covering it.

'What's that?' Paige asked.

'Have a look,' Phoebe answered excitedly as her sister unwrapped the blanket and saw a yellow eye, which stared at her.

She heard a loud, scared miaow followed by a long, scary hiss. Then as quick as lightning Magic dashed up the long, creepy, old stairs.

'Where are you Magic?' Phoebe cried wondering what her cat was up to. Suddenly Phoebe heard a big bang from in the haunted bathroom. So Phoebe crept in there and she saw a blurred black dash fly past her. So Phoebe followed her into the bedroom and Paige called out, *'Just use a spell.'*

So then Phoebe did a spell 'Abracadabra Findacadrabra,' Phoebe did as soon as she could.

Suddenly a swirl of sparkles and glitter formed like a hurricane in the bedroom then it went under the bed and all they saw was a big, shining, bright light. Then all of a sudden the cat came flying out from under the bed.

Paige got hold of Magic and took her down to the cauldron. Paige added newt's eye, bat's wing and last of all she added some fish heads, then she gave it to Magic to drink and Magic was never naughty ever again!

Rachel Sheath (12)
Swanmore Middle School, Ryde

The Life Of Tabatha Twitchet

Wednesday, best day of the week. Kids at school, adults at work and to make it even better, none of them will be back until five o'clock, thought Tabby as she skipped off her lavender-scented pillow onto the shiny kitchen floor. Breakfast was already out for her in her special bowl. *Umm, meat flakes,* thought Tabby.

She tried to plan her day in her head. First she would go for a stroll in the long luscious grass, then a nap under the apple tree for an hour. Then she might go on a rat and mouse hunt, just to make them even more scared. And after that more sleeping and strolling. Today was going to be a good day; she could sense it.

The air was warm, there was a slight breeze, but that didn't matter. The golden sun shone on Tabby's silky fur. Then the ground started to shake and grumble, it was Mrs Higgins, she hated cats, Tabby ran as fast as she could and when she got inside the safety of her home, she could hear the spitting noises that the lady made as she stormed back inside.

5 o'clock! What? She must have fallen asleep. She heard the door click and in they came. Soon the house was full of fun and laughter from the children. 'Purr,' went Tabby and she was asleep.

Kate Nutbourne (12)
Swanmore Middle School, Ryde

Searching Sri Lanka

20/01/05 - I'm on a helicopter making my way to Colombo City. I'm going to search tsunami's main victim; Sri Lanka.

21/01/05 - I've landed and I can already see disaster. People are crying. Children and parents are looking lonely, I really want to discover more. So I'm going to a town called Galle.

22/01/05 - As I approach Galle, I meet up with an American man who is an archaeologist. He has just started on Galle and first he is looking for goods from houses.

I've searched and I've found some amazing things. I've found some statues of animals (which look valuable), broken tables and chairs and some broken radios. We've also discovered some adult and babies' clothing, but they are ruined.

As I look over the horizon, later in the day, I see a group of children playing around. They don't have a clue where any of their family, homes or possessions are.

23/01/05 - I'm ready to start a day of discovery again. But today I'm flying in a helicopter to a town called Kandy. I'm visiting a refugee camp for the people whose homes are gone.

I'm at the camp and most of the children are looking quite happy. However, people that are about 15 years plus are either looking very glum or crying.

During the rest of the day I meet some people and talk to them about how they feel.

My journey is nearly done. I'm very pleased with what I have discovered, but touched with what I have seen; businesses ruined, people homeless and also people's lives completely wrecked.

Stacey Downer (12)
Swanmore Middle School, Ryde

A Day In A Different Life!
(My first day in the life of Cameron Diaz)

As I looked in the mirror I had long, blonde, wavy hair, with blue-green eyes. I was tall and quite skinny and I had a perfect figure. As I looked around the suite everything was all neat and in place.

There was quite a lot of expensive equipment in the room.

The next minute there was a knock at the door. 'Your limousine is waiting for you outside, and they are ready to take you to the studio whenever you're ready!' said the bodyguards as they entered the room.

As I walked outside there was paparazzi everywhere! People came up in my face taking pictures. The bodyguards took me safely to the limousine. When I got to the studio where they were filming Cameron Diaz's movie, 'The Sweetest Thing', I went to the dressing room where they did my hair and make-up it was so exciting!

Just before I was going to act, the director gave me a script, which I had to practise and know off by heart for when I was about to act. I loved being Cameron Diaz. It was the best day of my life, but it was quite stressful at times.

Letitia Mitchell (12)
Swanmore Middle School, Ryde

The Dark Wood

Clouds drifted over the distant hills as the school group shuddered from the cold. As the day went on the sun decided to come out and the trees cast shadows on the damp ground. The group stopped in a small clearing for lunch. Bangers and mash were served up onto makeshift plates. Before the group left, James nipped behind a tree. 'Ahh,' James said, relieved. Once he got back he noticed immediately … they had gone!

Panic ran up James' spine. 'Hello!' James yelled out. No reply. He pelted through the woods shouting out. Eventually he had to stop. He leant against a tree gulping in air. James was hungry so he bit into the sandwich he had with him. Tuna had never tasted so good.

James was running again. Already his legs were aching. He carried on, urging himself not to stop. He would eat his chocolate if he did. Daylight faded. James stopped in a confined clearing. There were wrappers and the grass was burnt from a campfire. 'The others have been here!' James exclaimed. He laid out his sleeping bag to sleep.

When he woke the sun was hidden behind the trees. He got up, packed up his stuff, ate the rest of his chocolate and started trekking again. After half an hour he could hear shouting. It was the others! 'I'm over here!' James called. Two of James' friends came out of the trees.

'Found you!' they shouted, laughing.

Phil Hodges (12)
Swanmore Middle School, Ryde

Report On The Tsunami

We landed at the main airport, the people who worked there had made a temporary airstrip, the wave had dumped debris all over the other runways and there was a man with two wooden planks signalling where to land. There was a child, she was crying, lots of pedestrians were crowded round comforting her.

I looked around, there was loads of wreckage, cars upside down, houses ripped clean apart but worst of all there were dead bodies washed up on the beach, some survivors crying, shaking as they were so cold and others searching in the rubble for lost relatives.

The sight was horrific. I almost felt myself cry, the helicopter landed. We were greeted by a soldier. In fact the whole Chinese army were there; the soldier guided us across the airspace and over to a tent. We entered the tent. There was a man sat in a chair smoking a pipe.

He asked what our business was. We said we were investigating the tsunami. He did not believe us so he asked the soldier to escort us back to the helicopter. We got back in and left Sri Lanka.

Elliot Winsor-Viney (12)
Swanmore Middle School, Ryde

Area 51

(15 years ago)

For many years scientists of America have been researching extraterrestrial activity. Sworn to secrecy these scientists have a tough life but one scientist rebelled. He thought that the world should know what was happening right under their noses and what was really out there so he video-recorded a diary. It included every aspect of his continuous research, from how he started to what his predictions were for the future of mankind. What he didn't know was that 15 years later a group of terrorists would discover this diary and unleash global destruction …

(Present day)

'I thought this place was quarantined,' whispered a special unit personnel to another, as he hastily stepped into the destroyed lift shaft. They observed their surroundings, searching for any slight abnormality. Everything seemed to look fine when suddenly someone spotted an open air vent. It had thick blood dripping from the inside. As they shone their faded torches into the vent something caught their eye. Before they could run to safety the creature attacked.

Fighting as hard as they could, blood spraying everywhere, they thought they were winning but the savage beast prevailed, ripping their beating hearts out of their chest, tearing off the people's limbs and stabbing them with it. Was this the end of the world as we know it or just a sick illusion?

James Dighton (12)
Swanmore Middle School, Ryde

The Story Of The Evil Fairy

Polly, the evil fairy, glided through the corridors of her bouncy castle.

Ha, ha, ha! she thought. *I'll take over the entire magical universe, but that nasty little fairy Esme better not try and stop me.* Polly was wearing a horrible pink poofy dress with lots of flowers. Polly and Esme had been enemies ever since they had an argument when they were best friends in fairy school.

'I'll work more on my evil plan tomorrow. Come on Smiff.'

Smiff was Polly's robot friend. Since she had no real friends, she had to make her own.

Yeah, evil plan, she thought. He didn't like Polly but he was programmed to stay with her all the time.

Polly went upstairs to get ready for bed. She was about to get into it when a dark figure emerged. It switched on the light which lit up a face.

'Baaah! Esme - I knew it!'

'Evil plan eh? Well we'll just have to see about that.'

Before she knew it, Polly was being tied down to the floor. Esme reached into her long coat's pocket and pulled out a fork. Down she went and scratched out Polly's eyes.

'Argh! Smiff! Save me!' Polly screamed breaking all the windows.

'No chance!' he smirked.

Next came the pliers. Esme gripped Polly's fingernails and pulled them up. 10 screams of pain echoed through the halls of the bouncy castle.

And that was the evil end of the evil fairy named Polly and her evil ways.

Becky Saxcoburg (13)
Swanmore Middle School, Ryde

The Teacher

The teacher starts its wave of destruction (daily activities) by crawling out of its cave and clawing its way into a scrappy piece of metal which is called an automobile. Wrapping its cold, dead-like fingers around the handbrake and slowly turning a cold, rusty key a great puff of black smoke explodes into the air and sends the automobile on its way.

Arriving at its main hunting ground the teacher smells the air. The teacher's main prey is the smaller and more vulnerable species, the child, which the teacher can smell a mile off. The teacher quickly gathers a small bunch of children and hordes them into a small, cramped room. Stuffing them all into chairs and tables it slaves them to write word after word for around six hours. It then releases the children, not physically harmed, but mentally. Retreating to a small room, which many teachers come to, they discuss matters with each other and to the dominant male (in other words the *headmaster!)* After many hours it returns home to rest for its next morning hunt …

Scott Wraxton (12)
Swanmore Middle School, Ryde

The Myth Of Jonny And The Jamberloo

Now we've all heard of Hercules and Pandora but compared to this myth they're all fairy tales, be prepared to be amazed as I tell the myth of the Jamberloo.

In the middle of the Indian Ocean there lays an island called Jamb which no man has ever returned from. Why? you say. It's because of the Jamberloo, the most hideous being that has ever existed, no one knows if it's man or beast. Some people say it rips its victims to shreds with its razor-sharp claws and it's covered in bloody tangled fur. Others say it has eyes as crimson as blood and is too terrifying for your worst nightmares. However there is only one man who knows what this tantalising beast is like and that's Jonny.

Jonny's an ordinary man whose father vanished on Jamb and when he turned 18 he decided to row his boat to the deserted island to see what this magnificent beast was. It was the most magnificent place he had ever seen, nevertheless that was all about to change. Steadily he pushed his way through the lush trees when suddenly he fell into darkness, moments later he was lying in a dingy cave.

He stood there in darkness, he could hear something breathing behind him, swiftly he spun round and saw the most horrific monster. No one knows how Jonny killed the Jamberloo, the only words he said when he got back were, 'My job's done!'

Megan Wingate (13)
Swanmore Middle School, Ryde

Weekly News

The council said there are an outsized, rapidly growing number of illegal immigrants entering the country and selling drugs or living illegally.

The people of the Isle of Wight are concerned and have complained about higher income to the immigrants who have arrived in Britain and less earnings for people who have lived in Britain all their lives and worked full time. The council are very confident the problem will reduce if the immigrants will pay a small amount of the income they get from the council back to the council, but the Isle of Wight police did not agree so they had a meeting.

The Isle of Wight and Hampshire police got together recently to discuss the dilemma. The outcome was very positive.

PC Smith has spoken to the newspaper about what will happen, he reports that they will resolve the trouble with the illegal immigrants by checking each and every one of the cars, vans or any source of transport before entering England and immigrants will pay tax for shelter.

The people of the Isle of Wight and Hampshire are very pleased by the conclusion and hope it will solve the difficulty with immigrants. The Isle of Wight council was not pleased though.

But the problem with drugs was discussed but no outcome was reached. The police will have another meeting next week and the problem will be resolved as soon as possible to stop immigrants selling drugs in the UK.

Poppy Yeo (13)
Swanmore Middle School, Ryde

A Day In The Life Of Amii And Becki On Friday Night

It was Friday evening and I was in my room with Power FM blaring out of my stereo. As I was deciding what to wear, my mobile rang. It was Becki. She wanted to know if I was still coming out with her that night. I said, 'Yes I will call for you at seven!' I put on my Playboy top and my skirt. Then I started doing my hair and make-up. It took me ages but I'd finally finished. I looked up to my clock and it was 7.10pm! I ran downstairs, put my boots on, got my handbag, and then got my dad to take me to Becki's house.

As we were walking down to the seafront to meet Christi, she phoned us and asked, 'Where are you?'

I said, 'We will be down there in five,' but on the way we met Sam and Will. When we got down there she had gone!

We were going to go to the ice rink but the manager wouldn't let me and Becki in so we all went bowling instead. I looked like a clown with my skirt and bowling shoes on! Sam and Becki thought it was really funny! And they couldn't stop laughing at me. I got a strike on my first go but Becki won the game! It was 10pm and my dad had come to take us home. So we said bye to the boys and went home.

Amii Stansfield (13)
Swanmore Middle School, Ryde

A Day In The Life Of A Salmon

Days after being born from his parents, Hubert Cumberdale the salmon was ready to start his adventure of riding up the great river.

Waiting for the right moment to start Hubert Cumberdale swam as fast as he could to get through the devastating current, swimming with his friends Margery Stuart-Baxter and Jeremy Fisher, on swimming upstream they were not shocked to see thousands and thousands of evil, mutated bears drooling over the tasty salmon.

After dodging a few bears suddenly, out of nowhere, a bear pounced on top of Margery Stuart-Baxter and shredded her head off her body and chewed her to miniature bites. After losing a friend Jeremy Fisher and Hubert Cumberdale managed to just about survive from the bears. Tired and weak they decided to take a quick rest to gain some energy. When Hubert awoke Jeremy was gone. Hubert started his adventure on his own, he met up with some other salmon and decided to go along with them.

After a while he got to a waterfall and saw a lot of dead bodies of those who had tried to get up. He saw Jeremy about to go up when Hubert caught him just before he jumped and told him they should jump together. As they jumped they almost made it, but then some salmon from below jumped and nudged Hubert and Jeremy. It gave them a boost and they managed to get up over the waterfall. When they got there they were too excited and Jeremy suddenly died of a heart attack. So Hubert Cumberdale went along to the nesting area to die shortly after with a bear eating him whole.

Robert Clark (13)
Swanmore Middle School, Ryde

A Day In The Life Of My Tortoises

I sit in the sun all of the day, until the sun has gone away. Mum and Dad are going out; they hope to go fishing for some trout. Immediately I try to get them to stop but as soon as I say it off they trot. I am upset and unhappy but here comes the rabbit, he is called Flappy. He's black and white and talks like a parrot; he hops a lot and likes to eat carrots. We play together for most of the day, until we are both put away. We toddle along as fast as we can; we try to hitch-hike on a van.

I feel so alone in this deserted place, but then I see a bright red face. The face of my owner happy and sweet, she's come outside to play with me. But what is this, a tray of water, something I'd never seen before. A horrid bath oh what a shock. Is that the time on my clock? I try to run but I don't get far, she's got me back now to the food bar. Lettuce, peaches, tomatoes and more, everything I want *galore, galore.* As I eat my dinner out of the corner of my eye, I see my family start to arrive. Now it's time to go to bed; time to rest our sleepy heads. I've had a weird day, good and bad, but now I'm back with my mum and dad.

Shelley Rickard-Worth (13)
Swanmore Middle School, Ryde

A Day In The Life Of Laura-Michelle Kelly (Mary Poppins)

What I think a day in the life of Laura-Michelle would be like: I reckon she has to get up early so she can have a big breakfast to start her up for her many performances. Then she travels to the Prince Edward Theatre for rehearsals and a sound check.

I also believe that she followed her dream and most definitely got to where she wanted to be!

Anyway after she has had her rehearsals and sound check she goes to get ready for her first performance. Whilst eating lunch she has her hair sorted then she gets her first costume on. Then she goes to make-up and then she is ready and raring. I decided to write a piece about Laura-Michelle because I am trying to follow my dream just like she did.

I wish to be a West End actress myself. Laura and my mum are the two people who have inspired me never to give up, so many thanks to them. I just hope I get there and thanks to you for reading this. I hope you enjoyed it. Thanks again.

Sadie Tompkins-McLean (12)
Swanmore Middle School, Ryde

Alien Abduction!

On Monday morning while children were on their way to school, a spacecraft stopped to hover above the town's park. The spacecraft scooped up a healthy schoolchild using a laser beam. For legal reasons the police have not released the name of who the child is.

Eyewitnesses have said that the aliens were purple with three eyes, four arms and eight legs. They have also said that the spacecraft is red with a green and white spotted bottom.

Police have released that they are missing a police helicopter that is looking for the spaceship. Police have warned the army and there should be street security by tomorrow morning.

Anyone with information about this horrific invasion should contact Ryde Police Station on 456789.

Police have said that if you need to leave your house, go with a friend.

Carl Everett (12)
Swanmore Middle School, Ryde

One Bright Summer's Day

One bright summer's day I saw a toad on the edge of the pond. I went to pick it up and I heard a hiss. I looked towards the left and saw a snake slithering towards me. I moved back and the snake made an S shape and leapt towards me but it leapt onto the toad. The snake dug its fangs in its neck and I ran indoors and got a pot to put it in and to keep as a pet. I put it in my shed and I fed it toads and insects.

That night a sound woke me up. I wondered what it was. It came from the shed, I didn't take any notice whatsoever so I went back to sleep. When I woke up and went down to feed the snake, I saw it lying in the corner of the shed and so I threw in a dead toad that I had found in the road.

I went indoors to have a bath and some breakfast then went to see the snake. I opened the shed door and looked at the snake. Something was different. I looked round then looked back. The snake had got bigger. It had grown a foot in half an hour. I wondered what breed of snake this was. A grow-a-foot-in-half-an-hour snake?

I went to feed the snake at 6 o'clock. The snake had grown another two feet. I wondered if I could make some money out of this snake - like showing people that there is a snake as big as a train. How big was it going to be in a week?

A week later it hadn't grown six feet. It had grown a foot and a half. And it had started to get aggressive towards people.

The next day on the news there was a report that there was a snake about, a dangerous one. The snake went into a school full of little children. It started to eat the children. Some of the children started to run out of the school and there was the army and CID plus the police force arriving to control the snake. By this time the snake had grown double the size it was at first. This meant that every time it ate something it grew a bit bigger each time. At that precise time there were about a hundred police and army at the scene. I wondered if they were going to kill the snake or if they were going to do tests and experiments on the beast. I wondered how many children it had eaten.

They thought they had killed it and they had taken the snake back to the lab to do some experiments on it when there was a movement in its stomach. Suddenly, there in front of my eyes, popped out another one and it started to eat the scientists one by one. Out of nowhere came a rock towards the snake and killed it instantly.

Daniel Sleet (13)
Sycamore Centre, Epsom

My Mobiles And Me
(An extract)

It was a hot bank holiday in April. I went with my friend Mark to the Carters steam fair. We were 15 at the time. We arrived there at 2.25pm. We could smell the burgers and chips, candyfloss and hot dogs with onions. It made my mouth water.

There were a lot of people, mainly groups of older kids. There was one group that stood out, who kept picking on people who were younger than them or smaller groups that would have no chance in a fight with them. We tried to stay out of their way, although later that day they started to pick on a friend, Miguel, who was 14 and who we had bumped into there. They started hitting him with rubber hammers and pushing him around, accusing him of picking on one of them. We knew this was not true, as they had said the same thing to other people. We got off the ride to help him, but straight away one of them said, 'Keep out of it Shorty, or we'll get someone to give you a kicking!' He was a large black lad of about 17 with black trainers and jogging bottoms, a red basketball shirt and a black leather jacket. He had a thick, heavy-looking gold chain round his neck and his hair braided closely to his head. He was quite a bit taller than me but very broad. I was dreading him coming over. I would have had no chance against him. I wanted to go home, but I stayed for my friend's sake.

As soon as we got there we looked around at all the rides. There was the octopus, the skids, dive-bomber, boats and a merry-go-round. As we were walking around, we could hear people screaming and they were very pale as if they were going to be sick.

It was very loud with all the shouting and all the music from the rides. The ear-splitting tune from the waltzers was deafening me on one side while the powerful thumping from the bass on the octopus was vibrating through me. The bright, blinding strobe lights, the flashing disco lights and the hard glare from the high-powered floodlights made people squint. The rides were quite fast. We went on the skids first. It was great. After that we went on the octopus, but the bar that held you in was very loose so I wasn't very happy with the ride.

When I got off, I walked over to the food and drinks bar and got a Coke. After that I went on the dive-bomber. It was very good but when it went backwards it made my stomach go.

After about an hour I went back on the dive-bomber but I lost my mobile phone and £10 so I went home because I was really angry.

At about half-past eight my cousin, Claire, phoned me at home and asked if I wanted to go to the fair again. At first I said I did not want to as I was still angry, but she said she would pay for me on a few of the rides, so I agreed. When we were younger, we used to spend a lot of time together but now she is always at work or out with her mates. She is 18 now and often I feel left out because she and my sister spend far more time together. Anyway Claire came and picked me up and we went back to the fair.

We went on the skids first and it was great with all the lights flashing and the music blasting in my ears. At first I was a bit put off by the screaming but after the first time I'd been on you could not get me off until Claire started feeling sick. When we got off, she was sick behind the caravans. She looked pale and had sick around her mouth, but she said she felt better. After a few more rides we watched the fireworks then we set off home.

James Stiff (16)
Sycamore Centre, Epsom

The Gypsy Tent

One summer's day me and my family went to Epsom fair. I looked around. There were all different stools and tents but one particular tent caught my eye, so I rushed over to it. I looked in. There was an old wrinkly lady sitting at a table. She had her fragile hands cupped over a green crystal ball. I walked in and in her quiet voice she said, 'Come in, the spirits are with us.'

I felt a shiver go down my spine.

She said, 'Don't worry my dear, the spirits won't harm you.' She started to rub her ball. Suddenly there was white writing that appeared over her ball. It said, 'Keep away from black horses or you will die'.

The next morning I woke up and my sister asked me to help her down the yard. I was on the way down there when I remembered what the gypsy had told me. I was feeling worried. I tried to forget about it but it kept flashing back into my head. I arrived at the yard and was feeling the same way as when I walked into the gypsy's tent.

My sister said to me, 'Are you OK because you are looking pale.'

I replied, 'I was just thinking about what the gypsy said to me yesterday.'

She said, 'I don't want to hear your soppy stories, now come and help me clean Darkness out.'

I had a funny feeling he was going to be that black horse I was supposed to be staying away from.

I built up my courage and went into the stable. He was black and my heart started to thump, I tried not to think about it but it as the only thing I could think about. I started to pick up the hay. I turned round to pick up the bucket with the food in when suddenly he kicked me in the face. I could feel the blood trickling down my face, cold and wet.

I opened my eyes to find out I was sweating in my bed and it had all been a nightmare.

Jack Gibson (13)
Sycamore Centre, Epsom

Getting Legless On A Lonely Saturday Morning

It was 10.30 on a Saturday morning, sunny and hot. Peter and I were outside McDonald's opposite the bike shop. We each had an opened can of Stella in one hand and seven in the other.

We were both 24. I was short with long purple hair, good-looking, wearing jeans, loafers and a blue Tommy Hilfiger shirt. My cousin, Pete, was the same age, very tall with short, black hair, wearing black jeans and a Ben Sherman shirt. The night before I had gone to the pub to have a quick drink after work on pay day. Then I had had a Chinese delivered to the flat. I live with my girlfriend, who stays at home looking after the baby. She is six months old with blonde hair - really cute, like her dad.

We had first met at school. She was new that day and I was attracted to her immediately. She had classic looks: she was small with long blonde hair and skinny legs. I was nervous to talk to her, but a week later I asked her if she would like to come to the cinema to see 'Bend It Like Beckham' and I was surprised when she agreed. The film was boring but we got on just fine. She had the same sense of humour, talked nicely and she seemed to feel the same about me.

As life moved on, we had a baby, got married and we have now been in the flat for two months.

So, why was I now on the street getting drunk with my cousin on a Saturday night? When I got home last night, we had a row about whose turn it was to change the baby's nappy. She asked me to but I was too tired as I had only just finished work and it had been a hard week, so I said, 'Do it yourself.' That was a bit harsh, and I wish I hadn't said it, but it is too late now. She got really upset, broke down in tears and said that I knew where the door was. I just got up, took my money and keys off the table, walked out and slammed the door.

This morning I woke up on the floor at Pete's. He lives with his mum in a maisonette near the Odeon cinema, but they don't have much space for me. I was embarrassed. I had a headache like the thumping of a loudspeaker. My mouth tasted as if I had smoked a thousand fags, dirty and dry. I felt really ill and thought I was going to throw up. I drank *eight* pints of water and felt a bit better.

I felt ashamed about last night, because I should have changed the dirty nappy. I rang Grace and tried to apologise, but she wouldn't have it. She said it was over for good and she didn't want to see me ever again. So, what else is there to do but drink?

Brett Carslake (15)
Sycamore Centre, Epsom

Keys From The Heavens?

It was just like any other morning, Dad was changing barrels and Mum was clearing tables before we opened. We had lived in pubs all my life and my parents seven years before that, strange things had always been happening, but this was the freakiest!

We were half an hour from opening and Mum needed the keys. She had a key rack where she always kept the keys, she shouted, 'Paddy get the keys.' I went to the rack but they weren't there. I went back to Mum and explained they weren't there, Mum thought Dad may have them with him, so I was sent to see.

I *hated* the cellar, it was so dark and creepy, and I always felt coldness on my neck. I shouted, 'Dad have you got the keys?'

'No son.'

I ran back to Mum who was in a worried state now because we only had 15 minutes left! We searched every room in the pub and flat, and it was impossible for anyone to take them as it was only me and my family in the pub!

Finally we had one last try; we all went outside to check the car park and suddenly, they just fell from the open air into my mum's hands! We weren't by any buildings or windows so no one could have chucked them. And to this day it hasn't been explained, but I know the truth, it was a *ghost!*

Patrick Coker
The Blandford School, Blandford Forum

One Cold Night In November

It was a cold night in November, when I was woken by a thunderstorm. I was lying in my bed staring up at the ceiling. I was thinking about the fact that I had to get up in three hours time to start my paper round. I closed my eyes and felt a draught by my feet, I tried to move them under the duvet but I could not move. I thought I had broken my back and I was paralysed or something. I opened my mouth to shout for help but nothing came out, just a hoarse whisper.

I heard what sounded like someone smirking and from the corner of my room a tall, dark shape came out, in fact it was more like a shadow and it did not look like it was walking, it was gliding towards me slowly but gaining in pace.

When it got to my bed it engulfed me in darkness then my chest got tighter and tighter. I had to close my eyes because they were stinging almost like when you get shampoo in them. Then my heart started pounding in my ears very quickly my chest was so tight now that I could no longer breathe. I lay there for the next 30 seconds trying to breathe as the overwhelming pressure built up, then everything stopped. I felt icy cold. I opened my eyes. The shadow had disappeared. It was over as quickly as it had started.

Nathan Kirby (14)
The Blandford School, Blandford Forum

Peace In Caroma

Heredes the tree demon dwells in his tree on Fanfare Hill. Sucking in the sweet air into his fiery lungs, scooping out his next victim. Patiently waiting. Still. The calm easy atmosphere so tranquil, so peaceful, destroyed by the ruckus of the village market. Heredes, wanting food swoops violently down into the crowd with his dagger-like claws glaring in the sunlight. Blinded by the sudden movement the villagers freeze. Heredes screaming with rage, lunges viciously at the crowd, elegantly yet dangerously. Within a second it is over. The people are killed. Heredes twirls back to his tree like a ballerina. He has successfully got the food. Heredes sits gorging waiting for his next prey.

Amadeus the great warrior of Genola hears the news. Amadeus decides something has to be done to bring peace back to Caroma. Even with power of an ox and speed of lightning he can't physically beat the beast. So he opts to use the beast's greed against him.

Amadeus comes out of where he has been hiding. He swiftly lays down two apples in front of Heredes' tree. One apple is fine the other bears a note reading, 'Do not eat' and contains poison. The beast appears outside his tree. Quickly he gobbles up the first apple. Unsatisfied he glances at the second. laughing to himself he eats the apple. Seconds later he lays dead. His greed overpowered his sense. Amadeus returns to Coroma market to tell the news. There is peace in Caroma again!

Ryan Keogh (14)
The Blandford School, Blandford Forum

The Legend Of Myhomiuss

Long ago, before Hercules and the Titans, lived a father, Myhomiuss, and his daughter, Yodudiuss. Myhomiuss loved animals, more than life. He had every single animal in the world until he heard news of a new bird. Myhomiuss booked to sail over to the island of Omilo to claim one, but there was a problem.

'But Father, I have my archery tournament then, you know how important archery is to me!' Yodudiuss cried.

'Yodudiuss, I've heard enough of your ranting; I'm going!'

'Father!'

'*Daughter!*' Myhomiuss roared and hit her round the head. He stormed onto the boat.

Yodudiuss lay holding her arrows. She held her cheek. 'Father ...'

The 'Inderhowse' had giant golden wings and a blue crown. Myhomiuss stared at its bright blue beak.

'*Bling-down,* bring me a blanket; I'm cold!' Myhomiuss boomed.

'Yes Sir!' the assistant whimpered and hurried off.

'Sir?'

'What?' Myhomiuss spat at another assistant.

'We've had terrible news; your daughter is dead ... she was hit with an arrow.'

'Never mind, there was always something wrong with her. She never liked pets ...' The disgusted assistant fled. 'Yes, go, I want to be alone with my pet!'

Myhomiuss grabbed the bird. It screamed and Myhomiuss felt suddenly sad, he felt sorrow for Yodudiuss. The bird flapped its priceless wings and dropped the greedy collector into a deep cavern. Bling-down watched as he fell. The bird transformed into the beautiful goddess of giving. Bling-down bowed as she winked with her perfect blue eyes.

Mike Wyatt (13)
The Blandford School, Blandford Forum

My Greek Myth

Prometheus, one of the great heroes of Greece, on approaching the cave of the Iraclops, one-eyed ogre of stone, froze untwitchingly and sniffed the air. A foul stench floated on the breeze. The pitch-black entrance to the cave loomed over him as he took his first few steps into it. The gloomy light began to fade as he probed deeper into the Iraclops' lair.

The cave, rank with fear, filled him with thoughts of battles, hatred long forgotten. He could feel the curse of the Iraclops getting stronger. Every step he took poisoned his mind more and more. He could feel the darkness drawing closer now.

Suddenly his thoughts turned to that which drew now close. He could now almost feel the piercing touch of his new found foe. Prometheus, in a moment of clarity, slowly, silently drew his sword. The now barely visible distant shard of light hit Prometheus' sword piercing into the eye of the Iraclops. Now blind the Iraclops froze. It let out a piercing scream bringing Prometheus to his knees.

Knowing that the Iraclops would soon come to its senses Prometheus took up his sword and thrust it into the darkness. The Iraclops fell silent. Dead. Prometheus lay still on the ground for some time. His sword, upon contact with the Iraclops had shattered leaving him with heavy wounds.

Some time later he brought himself to his feet and left the cave carrying with him the head of the Iraclops as proof of his triumph.

Kieran Davidson
The Blandford School, Blandford Forum

Pope Dies In Horror Fall!

Pope Benedict XVI has died from a fatal fall.

At 3pm on Tuesday 22nd May, the majestic Pope was very anxious about saying his first sermon to the expectant crowd at the Vatican. He was sat in his huge Tudor-style chair hoping his maiden lecture would impress the crowds. The astonishing previous Pope, John Paul II's speech was overwhelming.

The ancient architecture of the Vatican was filled to the brim with overexcited Catholics waiting to hear their phenomenal new Pope. The immense crowd were getting impatient, as they had been waiting for three agonisingly long days. The crowd's roar echoed around the Vatican's attractive walls.

The Pope had a sore throat therefore delaying the address.

A couple of minutes after 3pm, the Pope rose out of his chair and made his way to the glorious substantial steps. The Pope advanced down the steps to tremendous applause from the crowds. He was gliding down the steps as if flying when suddenly his agile foot slipped on the fifth Georgian fabric step. He fell extremely slowly, Matrix-style down the steps head first.

His followers were speechless and gobsmacked. There was an anxious never-ending silence. The crowds had just seen their leader, Jurgen Ritzenburg as some call him 'Papa Ritzi' die horrifically. They were shouting, 'Long live the Pope' moments before this horrendous event happened.

Some scientists believe that this might have been caused when a Boeing 747 crashed into the Atlantic Ocean affecting the Pope's pacemaker.

Henry Baggridge (14)
The Blandford School, Blandford Forum

No Way José

Queen rejects offer to become Mrs Morinuho

Today the Queen spoke out in disgust at José Moriniho as he asked her to marry him.

The Queen, aged just 56, was having a business meal with José when he popped the question.

'I just thought we were there to talk about the plans for his MBE, for services to sport, I was going to give him'.

José left early trying to avoid the press but came out to a riot. He looked scruffy and drunk whilst leaving the hotel.

It is now unsure whether or not José is in the right mind to take Chelsea to glory tonight, against the unstoppable AC Milan.

The royal butler Tim Bevington-King told the BBC, 'The Queen came back angrier than I have ever seen her. I think José should make a public apology to the Queen and the rest of the nation in order to win back the country's trust and, well, quite frankly the Queen's'.

Now it will be interesting to see if the Chelsea players fully back their manager through these difficult times.

There are may questions unanswered. One of which is will Roman Abromovic take action?

Tim Bevington-King (14)
The Blandford School, Blandford Forum

Arsenal Win FA Cup

It was a fine day at Old Trafford. The sun was shining and all the players were just about to start to sing the national anthem. The whistle went to start the match, Henry was already on the ball. 'He shoots … he scores.' Henry put away a great goal against Manchester United in the first two and a half minutes. Thierry Henry lobbed Roy Carol from forty-one yards. 13 minutes later Robert Pires scored a second goal for Arsenal. Man U's keeper should have been ashamed of himself.

The half-time whistle blew. Roy Keane and Ashley Cole were seen fighting in the middle of the pitch, the referee went over and gave Roy Keane a red and Ashley Cole only a yellow.

The second half started and a streaker came onto the pitch with 10 policemen chasing him. The whole game went quiet for about 20 minutes. Van Nistelrooy scored a volley from outside the box into the top corner, the crowd went crazy. Man U were back in it.

The game went quiet again when it was approaching full-time. The final whistle went. Arsenal went crazy. They'd won the FA Cup for the fifth time. Alex Ferguson had something to say. 'This referee was against us. He should have given Cole a red card because he started it. If you didn't have Cole we would have won, I am going to put an offer on him for next season'.

Wasn't that a great match!

Richard Hoyt (13)
The Blandford School, Blandford Forum

The New Arsenal Stadium Burns!

Yesterday morning in London the new Arsenal stadium caught alight while manager Arsene Wenger and Chelsea midfielder Claude Makalele were having a meeting about a possible move to Arsenal. Makalele just got out and with serious injuries, but unfortunately Arsene Wenger died.

The London police are holding an enquiry into how the fire happened. There have been reports that a bunch of Liverpool fans were outside the stadium on the night the fire happened. What Makalele was doing there we don't know, but if Arsenal made an illegal bid for him then Arsenal could have points deducted, then they could face relegation this season.

In other news Manchester United have signed Italian striker Fernando Cavenaghi for £9 million. Also Champions League top scorer Andriy Scheuchenko could be out for 10 months after breaking his pelvis in Milan's 2-1 win over Sparta Prague.

Dario Roncaglia (14)
The Blandford School, Blandford Forum

Manchester United Sign Beckham?

Yesterday a scene of events occurred from Alex Ferguson getting sacked to Manchester United getting Beckham.

Alex Ferguson was sacked yesterday when Manchester United lost 5-3 to Arsenal in the FA Cup Final. The board of directors believed he lost the match on purpose for a bribe from Arsene Wenger.

The FA are investigating this crime, and the result of the enquiry will be the return or fall of Alex Ferguson.

At the moment, Roy Keane (Manchester United midfielder) has taken over the role as player-manager.

There are a lot of applications for the managerial position, but if Roy Keane retired and focused on his managerial career, he would be appointed without a doubt.

Arsene Wenger is also being investigated to see if he bribed the ex-Manchester United manager in the FA Cup Final.

One of the Arsenal players has come forth and given us news of his manager's wrongdoing.

'He has been meeting with the board director a lot lately and has met with Alex Ferguson twice before the match'.

Although the player remains unknown, the interview will still be used as a crucial part of the evidence.

Beckham revealed that he is pleased to be back at Manchester United and now he can concentrate on his football career without the stress from Alex Ferguson.

New manager, Roy Keane, is in talks with youngster Freddy Adu, who he's had his eye on, but Manchester United won't be able to sign anyone until these matters are sorted and they are back to normal.

Courtney Samways
The Blandford School, Blandford Forum

Body Found In Forest . . .

Police are investigating the discovery of a woman's body in a forest near Swanage.

On Tuesday afternoon Megdown Forest at Ullwell, Swanage, was sold to the Lace family for £5,000.

Immediately after the sale was completed, the family, middle-aged parents with their teenage children, decided to walk through the forest to see what it was like.

'We were expecting to find plants and wildlife in our forest, but we were shocked to find a dead body instead,' 45-year-old Bob explained to our reporter.

Next to the unidentified body was a black cat with green eyes. The cat was sitting beside the body staring at the Lace family as if it was protecting it. The family immediately phoned the police to report the death.

When the police arrived, the cat was still sitting staring, the police tried to identify the body but could not. They taped off the area around the body and called MIT. The Murder Investigation Team took the body away for tests. 'We have no idea who this body belongs to,' Detective Inspector Silva said.

As the van pulled away from the scene, the cat suddenly disappeared. The family were left to try to find out where the cat had gone, they are currently printing leaflets in the hope that someone will recognise the cat and help the police to solve this mystery.

Craig Sutherland (14)
The Blandford School, Blandford Forum

Liberation Of Europe And The Bravery Of Soldiers In Normandy

We took off from out main ship into the landing craft which wobbled like a buoy. We set off towards the shore of Normandy, my fellow squad throwing up over the side. In the distance I could see the cliffs, white cliffs, and down below the sight of pill boxes and many landing craft overturned.

It started to hit me, we would be going there into a sacrifice where men would lose their lives. A shot came and hit the front of the boat. My wits came about me and I started to shake whilst trying to load the bullets into my cartridge.

'2 minutes,' he shouted, giving us the warning that we would be hitting the beaches soon.

Before I knew it the ramp was down and we were running for cover in craters made by artillery guns. I lay there for a while getting my breath back, looking around me at the dead bodies and the medics trying to help the injured soldiers.

I took out my sniper rifle and aimed the sights, then put the cartridge into the gun. I peeked my head over the top and saw a German machine-gunner picking off our men by the dozen. I picked up my rifle and aimed at the man. *Bang!* The gunner was out and one of the Canadian soldiers went and threw a grenade into it. After all that I can truly say that I helped win WWII and the liberation of Europe from Nazi rule.

Justin Hall (14)
The Blandford School, Blandford Forum

50 Years Of Waiting Is Over -
A Day In The Life Of José Mourinho

One game, one win, the prize? The Premiership title.

Today, I, José Mourinho, have the chance to make history, to make my team, Chelsea, winners of the English League for the first time in fifty years. The trip up to Bolton was a nervous one, but who knows what the reaction would be if the victory was assured.

We had arrived, along with the fans, at the Reebok Stadium. As the fans took to their seats, the players, Mr Abramovich, and the staff, including myself, took to the dug-out area. The match began. The nerves came back again, but the display I was seeing was like no other I had seen so far this season. This display was not up to standard. There was nothing we could do until half-time.

The half-time whistle went and Mr Abramovich was less than impressed, so we, all the staff, walked down the tunnel to the changing rooms.

After the team talk, the players knew what was required of them. Forty-five minutes, one goal could seal the title. The referee blew his whistle to start the second half. The team started to play a part in the game. It wasn't until quite late in the game until Frank Lampard came into the Bolton penalty area and slotted it past the keeper. At last it was 1-0 and the title was in sight. About ten minutes later, Lampard again shot into the penalty area, placed it past the keeper, 2-0, the title was ours. The final whistle went, the party began. My job was done.

Neil Chivers (14)
The Blandford School, Blandford Forum

Is It Good Or Bad Luck That Comes In Threes?
(An extract)

Sandra woke to the smell of a thousand fires. As her eyes adjusted to the darkness, she saw black smog whistle down the landing.

No, it couldn't be, could it? Yes it was, her house was on fire. She dashed out of her room, grabbing her cardie on the way.

'Dave, Dave, get up quick, the house is on fire.'

Dave was her 17-year-old son; short and stumpy, just like his dad, yet thin for his size.

Dave ran downstairs aiding his mum on the way. By now the house was practically ash, it crumbled around them. As they reached the front door, the stairs collapsed.

They were now outside and a crowd had gathered. They watched their house fall.

It may have seemed pretty devastating at the time, but they soon got their lives back on track; they moved in with Sandra's auntie, their lives were going pretty well.

In fact, Dave had got engaged to his long-term girlfriend, Debbie.

It hadn't always been plain sailing for Debbie and him. Stuart, Dave's so-called best friend and neighbour, accused Dave of stealing Debbie from him. They had a couple of fights but nothing came of it, yet Sandra thought her son's engagement to Debbie would cause some friction between Stuart and Dave, so she told Dave not to tell Stuart and he agreed.

Dave didn't always keep to his word and between them, Dave and Debbie decided to tell Stuart that they were going to get married. I won't say why yet, but luckily for Dave, his mum had been listening in on his conversation about telling Stuart. She followed him round to Stuart's house next door and waited outside, hidden behind a bush. She saw the whole conversation through the kitchen window, yet she didn't expect to see Stuart furiously grab for a knife in the drawer and plunge it into her son's chest.

She let out a silent cry as her young son fell to the floor of a murderer's kitchen …

Katie Shorto (14)
The Blandford School, Blandford Forum

A Day In The Life Of Percy

Pigeons are the kings and queens of all bird tables. Although we often get fed in gardens, you still have to find the garden. So I am going to show you how hard it is being me.

First, off to Mrs Drew's garden. The old woman leaves stale breadcrumbs, why can't it be fresh just once? She often spills her problems to me, like they burst out of her from being cooped up too long, while she watches me eat. You have to be quick on your feet here as the blue tits, or blue twits as I call them, can eat very quickly!

If it is spring I then fly to the farmer's best crop field. I don't know why humans haven't tried flying yet; you call yourselves the top of the food chain, we are the real tops. We can go anywhere we please. Although I have to stop to rest in trees every few minutes, the only problem is that the trees are not strong enough, so I often bend them.

Usually, in spring, farmers are ploughing seeds so I go and have a little snack before moving on. The seagulls swarm around the field too but I usually get through. They are more stupid than they look - they aren't even near the sea!

It's not all hard work; you always have lots of friends. Although they all look the same so it's hard to remember names.

Hannah Garrett (13)
The Blandford School, Blandford Forum

A Day In The Life Of …

I thought he was my friend. Friends don't do this to you. My life used to be the same as everyone else's, but now it's ruined by someone I thought I could trust, someone who cared enough to pay me back for my good deeds. He didn't really mean it. Maybe he hated me. Every day used to be different but now it's the same.

Day in, day out, I see cold, blank walls. I sleep in the same room as someone who is never going to be free. Free like I should be, as I'm innocent. Out there somewhere I know my family is breaking. Breaking like glass. They have nothing. I have nothing. Every day in the morning I awake, knowing that it is going to be the same as yesterday - do my chores at 6am, eat half cooked food. It's a slave camp. Yet, I know I'm innocent.

Why won't anyone believe me? Maybe it's just a dream that I can't get out of. Sitting on the bed, hard and cold like an ice cube, I think. Thinking that is destroying my brain. But I still know I'm innocent. Every night I dream of a peaceful world, a world where everyone has their say, a world where everyone can live their life.

Outside somewhere I hope someone believes me. That I'm innocent. Someone tell them. I'm innocent. Believe me, I'm innocent. Tell them I'm innocent. Only I can't tell them here in this cold, lonely prison cell.

Zoe Greenfield (14)
The Blandford School, Blandford Forum

Don't You Just Hate Healthy Food?

Don't you just hate healthy food shops? They look, smell and even taste healthy. I despise healthy food. You know, all the cod liver oils and things like prunes covered in yoghurt, which really means shrivelled-up plums covered in fake white chocolate! Who would eat that? I have to live in a healthy food shop! It all started with Mum.

'John, get down here. I have an idea!' Mum called. 'Oh Hayden, there's no point trying to run away, you can hear it too!'

Dad walked in and we all sat around at the old kitchen table. Mum had that look in her eye when she was about to shout, give us a long lecture or she needed to borrow something. We got the lecture! She rambled on and on and on!

'We are spending too much ... blah, blah, blah. I'm already working too long hours ... blah, blah, blah. I have rung around and ... blah, blah, blah. I have found that if I start up a health food stop I would ...'

Dad and I seemed to wake up.

'A health food shop! Are you mad? Nobody would buy from a health food shop.'

'Do you know how much I would get jipped! Mum, I refuse to co ...'

'Look Hayden, if you would let me finish, then you would know that we would move. Don't say anything, yet! Up to where Grandma lives as she's getting old. Also we would have more room as we will have a house with a shop at the front not just a bungalow. We will have a bigger garden, larger rooms and a lot more money,' Mum said softly, but in a voice that you wouldn't want to mess with.

Who could refuse? A bigger room? That might not be a bigger deal to you, but mine is like a cardboard box. Well, it all fits in four of them! And that's how my old life ended with no friends or family around, and my new life started with lots of new friends and my stinky grandma. Well you can't have it all! Well, my new friends were ducks. OK, real friends? Do people who chuck raisins at you count? So, to be honest, my life just got worse!

Harriet Cunningham (13)
The Blandford School, Blandford Forum

Stories And Fiction

People say that mummies are cursed, but not a lot of people believe it. But what if I told you that a mummy sunk one of the most famous ships in the world? Yes, I am talking about the Titanic. And yes, there was one aboard the ship. Maybe I've already lost you, but what if I told you that people started dying before the accident? Have I got your attention? Good! Now I can tell you all I know.

There was this one lady, she wasn't young anymore, and when you looked in her eyes, you couldn't see any life in her. She was dressed all in black like she was going to a funeral. No one knew her name. That might be one of the reasons why she scared people so much, they would walk in the other direction when they saw her. Rumours started going round the ship, but only one of them was true.

She sat in the cargo bay all day after breakfast and if she saw anyone within 20 metres of the sarcophagus they would get a visit from her and no one else would see them again. They were probably chucked overboard along with all the binoculars on board.

No one knows why she did it but most people thought she was possessed. I believe that she was. She certainly looked it.

You can believe what you want to, but a lot of people were killed and some of them were brutally murdered. I'm telling you this so that hopefully you will think twice whenever you see someone suspicious, near where a mummy is.

Marie Christine Cowgill (13)
The Blandford School, Blandford Forum

A Day In The Life Of Football Boots

I think it's a nice day out today because there's light peeping through the bottom of the door. I get ever so lonely in this cupboard. There are other football boots in here but they all think they're better than me, especially those Adidas Predators, just because they have a pull down tongue and a lot of power. Well, I have a hidden lace-up system and I am lighter than they are.

Here comes Billy, I hope he picks me because I never get to kick a ball anymore, he always picks those Adidas Predators. I miss kicking the ball. I love it when it just glides through the air into the back of the net and the sound of the smash when you hit.

Oh yes, he's picked me. Oh, it tickles when he ties my laces up. It is a wonderful day out, the green grass with drops of dew on, the sun blazing and the clear blue sky. I love taking free kicks, you take a few steps back and run up and smash the ball into the back of the net. It makes a nice sound when it hits the net. Penalties are the worst. It stings when you kick the ball too hard.

Oh no, it's starting to rain and the ground will get all muddy. I hate it when my nice, clean, smooth leather gets all dirty, then I have to get cleaned. Now it's back to the cupboard again, I suppose.

Harry Eves (14)
The Blandford School, Blandford Forum

A Day In The Life Of A Born-To-Be-Perfect Girl

Hi, this is me, Roxanne. I live in London in a big townhouse. Mother is a lawyer, Father is a solicitor, and I am an only child.

Every day I wake up, peel my avocado face mask off and go into my luxury bathroom.

At 7.05 I wander downstairs where my bowl of Special K is waiting, prepared by Bobby, the butler. He is such a great butler, he even packs me a low carb diet lunch for school.

At 8.35, Sid, my chauffeur, pulls up to school in my new limo that Daddy got me for my birthday. All the other girls stare with funny looks on their faces. Mummy says they're jealous and I should never pull a face like that as the wind may change!

First lesson, maths. I get into my seat and Mrs Barnwell collects my homework in. Bobby does the writing and Mummy helps me dictate it to him.

At break time I often go to the library or if it's nice, I sit under my sunshade I bring from home and read a book.

Later when I get home from school, Kieran, my karate teacher, helps me learn some new self-defence routines. Daddy says I have to know how to protect myself. Then I cool down and unwind whilst playing Mozart on the grand piano in my room.

Towards bedtime, Martha, the maid, applies my new face mask and curls my hair ready for the morning.

Well, I hope you have enjoyed my day, I'm off to have supper in the grand hall now. Bye.

Jess Ryall (14)
The Blandford School, Blandford Forum

Butterflies In My Belly

Another fantastic day of my holiday. Today we're going jet-skiing.

We arrived at the location and there was a large, tattered, sheet-like thing. We opened the creaking, decaying door. A tatty, hard core-looking man was sitting down at his desk smoking a cigar with a magazine grasped in his hairy, cut hands. The man introduced himself, his name was Matty. He asked us to sign insurance papers and the rest of it and he went out and introduced us to the jet-skis. It was a totally different environment, it looked so modern all these jet-skis lined up like a little boy's toy soldiers.

We finally got on the jet-skis and in the water. We zoomed out of the bay and went about 200m out to sea. Suddenly I saw these fins circling around in the water. I was alarmed. My dad and sister were behind. I did not say anything so I did not alarm my sister who was dreadfully scared of sharks.

Suddenly the fins swam towards us. As they came closer, I thought, *these sharks are awfully small.* Suddenly it dawned on me that they were dolphins! They started swimming under the jet-ski! I felt like I was being picked up by the butterflies in my belly fiercely trying to escape from my stomach. It was an amazing experience. The dolphins looked so elegant in the water, the sun was gleaming on the top of their bodies making them look like shooting stars thrusting themselves through the sky. The dolphins then fled as if the lord of the sea was calling them.

Christian Swann (13)
The Blandford School, Blandford Forum

Past, Present And Future

It isn't very often that my family comes round to mine, so when my daughter offered to cook dinner, I naturally accepted.

'Grandma! Look what we've found!' My grandchildren, Lilly and Becky bounded in, holding a dusty box.

'I forgot I had that old thing.' I reached out for the box. 'Look, it's me and your grandad at Weymouth beach!'

'You have real teeth there Grandma!' Becky remarked.

I smiled. Seeing Arthur reminded me of the confusing thing that happened all those years ago.

'Who's that man? He looks all smeared and you can hardly see him,' Lilly said.

'I'll tell you, but you won't believe me,' I said. 'I barely believed it myself.'

'Tell us!'

'Well, it was back in 1952 and your grandad and I had just begun courting. We went to stay in a holiday cottage at Weymouth.' I took a deep breath. 'The weather was hot and we went for a walk along the beach. Your grandad had left his sunglasses at the cottage, so I waited for him at the ice cream van.'

'More, more!'

'Alright. So I was sat on a bench and I saw an old friend. We were sat chatting and reminiscing about old times and what could have been, and then Arthur came back. For some reason he completely ignored Brian. I introduced them and Arthur just asked me who I was talking about. Brian was still sat there but Arthur could clearly not see him. Suddenly, Brian disappeared and, confused as I was, I just put it to the back of my mind.'

'Spooky,' Lilly whispered.

I nodded in agreement. 'And later that day, when we arrived back at Blandford, my friend Maria told me that Brian had killed himself not long after I turned him down.'

'So he was like … a ghost?' Lilly shuddered.

'I'll never know, but when Arthur died a year later I felt like I'd lost the second half of my heart. My part for him, and my part for Brian …'

Emma Damon
The Blandford School, Blandford Forum

A Day In The Life Of The Grim Reaper

Today I have already killed 3 people; an old couple who died together and a little boy. Killing the little boy got me on a real downer as he had only been alive for 8 years and the old couple had been on the planet for 80. The child was only just starting to enjoy life.

I don't like my job as I have to kill people for a living, but I have to do it otherwise the planet's population would spiral out of control. This is a major factor for me sticking to my work, as no one else would do this job.

I get very tired and sweaty carrying around my scythe and wearing my thick, heavy, black cloak. I work with the Devil and hate him. He makes me scratch his back and makes me do all of his dirty work. It is a shame that he can't be killed, as I would love to kill him with my scythe and make him pay for all of the nasty things he does to the dead souls that are in the river of Hell.

I enjoy a beer in the evening while watching the footy. I support Liverpool and that is why the referee gave the goal against Chelsea as I said to him that if he gave them the goal then I wouldn't kill him. I enjoy going out and meeting the other Grim Reapers.

Tom Cox (14)
The Blandford School, Blandford Forum

The Object Of The Escape

Rowanne sipped the half drunk glass of red wine while staring at the loaded black object lying in front of her. *Ring, ring.* She picked up.
'It's time.'
She clutched her handbag and the black object, then made her way out of the building and onto the streets. It was a cold, bitter night, just right. She walked round the corner catching a glimpse of the passenger seat as the car drove past. She stopped. Stood in front of her was a tall figure hidden under clothes. She took out an object she had hidden in her coat. She passed over the packet and walked away. She gripped hold of the other object. She knew around the corner there was a car and someone waiting, waiting for her. How was she going to pull it off?
She took out of her handbag a red headscarf and wrapped it on. Carrying the object tight in her hand, she tucked it in her coat. A car was approaching, she waited until it got nearer. She struck out at the driver and held the gun to his head. She pulled the man out and told him to walk on as normally as he could. She slid into the car and drove off. As she approached the building, she saw a black car similar to the one before, and stopped the car.
By the next morning, she had disappeared, she had escaped.

Laura Dewhurst (14)
The Blandford School, Blandford Forum

The Lady And The White Horse

It was a midsummer's day and Lucy was walking down the lane, enjoying the sunshine. Then suddenly she heard a dog barking. She turned to her right and saw a woman who had short brown hair tied back in a knot. She seemed to be surrounded by a cold mist. Lucy shivered.

'Hello, my name is Roberta White,' she said. She was on a horse.

'Hi ... I'm Lucy. Your dog and horse are cute. Are you taking them for a walk?'

'No, just out hunting foxes.'

'Oh ... but isn't hunting banned? You're not supposed to hunt foxes anymore,' Lucy replied.

'Oh, I've never heard of this insane rule, I will go talk to my father about this. Me, Spark and Cherry come here every night,' Roberta said.

'Well, I better go ... bye,' Lucy replied. She looked in front of her, then back again.

Roberta was gone and the sun had risen again. Lucy made her way back home.

'Hi love, where did you go?' her mother asked.

'Just up the lane. Met a woman called Roberta White,' Lucy replied.

'Don't lie, Lucy!' her mother said.

'I'm not lying Mum, she was out hunting with her dog and horse,' Lucy replied.

'Roberta White died twenty years ago, Luce, she tried to jump a gate on her horse and broke her neck while fox-hunting.'

'But I just had a conversation with her, seriously.'

Lucy went to the library and saw that it was true. Had she really seen the ghosts of Roberta and her horse?

April Orchard (14)
The Blandford School, Blandford Forum

The Awoken

A few years ago, I held my dad's hand in one hand and my belongings in the other as I walked into my new house. This wasn't a normal house, this was different.

As I walked around my house I saw pictures of people on the wall. One said, 'James Smith 1900-1968'. He'd died on my birthday. As I stared at the picture I heard the fireplace crackle and the footsteps of my father.

As I laid down in my room staring around the room, my dad came in. He told me he was going to pick up the last bit of furniture. As I was tired he told me to get some sleep. These were the most feared words that my dad could have said. I heard the door close. I also heard footsteps outside my room. I hadn't eaten all day. My stomach was rumbling. The kitchen was two floors down. I was afraid to leave my bed.

I tried to ignore all this. I turned my alarm on and went to sleep. I was woken by my alarm at 3am although my alarm was set for 9am. I turned it back on. It happened again at 4am. At this point I was getting scared. I was lying there and I tried to move to get a glass of water but I was pinned to my bed. All of a sudden I was lifted, then thrown across my room. I saw an object fly towards the door. It went straight through.

I couldn't call anyone, nobody was in the house. I was afraid. I was alone.

Jaz Arwand
The Blandford School, Blandford Forum

Dreamer

There she is, walking past with her girlfriends, impressing every boy and even the girls as she walks through the middle of the playground. Every girl admires how beautiful she is and all the boys just whistle at her. Before now, I've always dreamed about her being mine, but now it's changed. For nine months, I've had to see her with three different boys, and just get a 'Hi' whenever I see her, but now it's my turn. Me and her together at last. Finally I've been given a chance, and now I know what it's like to be with her all the time. But the feeling is indescribable, it's impossible to put into words. Whenever I look into her eyes and we connect, I just feel like I'm on top of the world.

It's amazing how easily my life can just change. Before, it was just nothing, but now it's everything. To me she's amazing, nothing compares at all. To other boys, she has bad points and things that make her unpopular, but I don't see them; anything I see is just unexplainable. We're so good together as well, we make each other laugh all the time, and she's really the only girl that makes me laugh. I've never been as happy as I am with her and just can't believe that I used to be a 'dreamer'. I'll try my hardest to get just the one chance that I deserve.

Rory Loxton
The Blandford School, Blandford Forum

A Tale Of Resolve

Hester, a young scullery maid, was a plain woman, ordinary but for her spirited nature and intense desire that was so evident in her auburn eyes.

She had longed desperately for a sense of security, which she had yearned for ever since her parents abandoned her in that devastating civil war. She had never escaped that dismal, gaping wound in her heart. Now was her chance, and seize it she would.

She had found, at last, that love in the heart of that blacksmith, Harry Brown. They were inseparable, closer than two peas in a pod. Skiving from shoeing countless cart horses and skipping seamless scrubbing to meet each other with overflowing, boundless hearts.

But as always in such soul-wrenching tales, dear reader, there is a catch. Hester and Harry were as poor as church mice, surviving only on scraps from their generous mistress. There was not even money enough for an engagement ring, let alone a wedding. After much debate, they settled on one ominous solution, the only way out of a vicious circle of poverty.

As Hester's heart ricocheted within her ribcage like a wild bullet, her eyes fastened furtively on a stash of exquisite silver in the pawnbroker's clumsy chamber. Clutching the treasure, she hastened from the scene, breathlessly finding Harry's comforting arms.

With a brief, helpless glance at each other, they thrust the silver tangle into the glowing furnace. Shaping their future, Harry moulded a ring and sifted it from the dying ashes.

Verity Ockenden (13)
The Blandford School, Blandford Forum

A Game Of Two Halves

The whistle had blown and the match had started. The fans were restless and the game had begun. It was Ansville and Stoke United. Freddy Shoc was the star player for Ansville, and he was off. Freddy ran down the pitch, crossed the halfway line and was off. He ran, and then out of the blue, Andrew French slid in with a brilliant tackle. These two had an unhealthy resemblance. 'Good tackle,' Freddy said, helping him up from the ground. Andrew just winked and got back into position.

Ansville now had the ball and their players were on the run to goal, when they got tackled, and then a defender cleared the ball. Freddy chested the ball down and took a shot; the keeper dived too soon, but Andrew was there again with a clearance off the line. Then the whistle blew for half-time.

The second half started and the game was back on. Freddy had the ball again and was running; this time he got tackled by Andrew and Andrew ran and went for the goal, shooting just from halfway and coming just off the cross bar. The crowd sighed with relief.

'So close,' he mumbled to himself and carried on playing.

Freddy had the ball and another player came in with a poor sliding tackle. The ref sent the player straight off. Andrew spoke to the player. He went over and apologised. This was unusual for players from two other teams to be such friends on the pitch.

They were in the final minutes and Freddy ran and shot. It swerved in and Andrew was over the other side of the ref. The ref blew the whistle and the score was 1-0. Freddy and Andrew swapped shirts and went to their teams. 'See you later, bro.'

Elliot Edwards (13)
The Blandford School, Blandford Forum

The Day The Yeti Came To Town

'Argh!' everyone was screaming and running up away from town.
Boom! Crash!
'Run for your life, the yeti is coming!'
'Don't be silly,' I said, just standing there. 'The yeti lives in Alaska.'
'Well not any more, look out!' shouted a local resident.
Then appeared the huge white monster. *Roar!* It noticed me though, and stopped. I stood there looking up at it, and it staring down at me.
'Mumph!'
I think he's puzzled, he hasn't got the guts to squish me, but he needs to, to get through. Then I said to him, 'Come with me.' So off we went.
We eventually ended up in an abandoned car park, it was very quiet. I asked the yeti, 'Why are you here?'
'I need a new home, my other one melted.'
'Well, I'll help you to find a new one to live in.'
'OK, then,' the white monster replied.
So off we set once again, but this time away from town and all of the destruction. We went into a mountainside where there was a cave carved out. It was just big enough to fit the Abominable Snowman in, and because it was on the side of a mountain, it was quite cold so he could survive.
So we said our byes and off I travelled back down the mountainside. It was quite a long walk back, but that was OK, and when I did eventually get back, I saw that the people were rebuilding the town.

Nathan Jeffries (14)
The Blandford School, Blandford Forum

Swarmed

Christian was walking through the woods when he passed out. He awoke a few hours later in a net on the floor with a little man, gagged, next to him. There was a loud noise from behind and they noticed a lot of people with masks and spears. Off to their right they noticed a tall man leaning against a tree, wearing goggles and a long trenchcoat, and battle cries filled the air from the masked savages.

Then the loud noise came again, the savages quickly silenced and ran away.

The tall man cut Christian and the little man free and removed the gag, and to his amusement, the little man started attacking Christian, so the strange man pulled out his revolver.

The noise started again. Christian looked at the little man and there was a clean hole through his forehead - and the tall man and Christian walked away.

The next morning, Christian woke up and the man wasn't there. He started to panic, but then the man arrived with a bag of fruit and a flask of water. Over breakfast the man explained everything.

The gunslinger and Christian hit the road again. As soon as they reached a clearing, they were swarmed by zombies and the gunslinger knew who was there because he had escaped the dark lord's dungeons before.

The loud shots sounded again.

Matt Veal (13)
The Blandford School, Blandford Forum

A Day In The Life Of …

I woke up. I looked around. It was a dark, hot cell or jail. I had been placed underneath red-hot poles, just inches away from me. Was this a torture cell? It felt like one. I was getting a tan! My body was rising and inflating and I was really burning.

Suddenly, I was taken out by a fluffy material and put on a cool surface. My body was being shoved into a huge hole by two pink claws. Huge white pillars were closing in on me and crushing everything in their path. My lifeblood was oozing everywhere. As my backbone crunched, I squealed. Walls were closing in, forcing me backwards down a giant dark tube. I landed in green water in a big cave. The green water spat like fire and burned much of my skin. It wouldn't stop burning. I looked around for an escape and then saw another person.

'What is this?' I asked.

'It's a massacre,' replied the nearly dissolved person. 'This room shoots out acid,' he said. 'There is no escape, many of my friends are already dead.'

'What can we do?' I asked.

'There is nothing we can do!' he exclaimed.

More acid shot out and burned the lower half of my body. My companion had become mush on the floor. This time a lot more shot out and most of my body was gone. A tube opened up. The last thing I remember was falling down, down, down …

Tom New (14)
The Blandford School, Blandford Forum

The Signalman

I always liked visiting my nan; she used to make toasted muffins on her fire and she let me heap on loads of home-made jam, which my mum would have told me off about at home. Her house was always pristine and it was always nice to sleep in one of the beds she had prepared. In her room for guests, she'd always have a massive double bed covered in home-knitted blankets. But this stay was to be unlike any other stay before, I was to discover a disturbing secret about their house.

I was talking to my grandad today about the house, by the roaring fire. I discovered that their house used to be an old railway station.

That night I was settling into bed. I was just about to close my eyes, then I suddenly heard loud thuds. It sounded like Grandad had got in late from the pub again, so I got out of bed and went to the stairs, but no one was there. So I got back in bed and then they started again. I tried to ignore them, but they just got louder and louder.

The next morning I got dressed quickly and went straight to the library. I found out that there was a terrible accident on the railway where my nan's house is. Over 300 people died because the signalman didn't get to the track quickly enough. Maybe that was him running up the stairs to where the train tracks were ... ?

Kieran Tickner-Hinkes (13)
The Blandford School, Blandford Forum

The Lost Boy

The bare trees towered over him as he shivered in the cold night air. It was pitch-black, spare the pittance of light his torch gave. All he heard was the occasional tree groaning in the wind. He looked around, it couldn't be far now. His torch flickered and went out; he threw it on the floor in frustration. It was total darkness now. As he moved on through the night, he started to feel weary, but he knew he couldn't fall asleep now, not now that he was so close.

An eerie moon appeared from behind a dark cloud, the wood now flooded with pale light. He was grateful for the change and felt slightly encouraged.

He began to get the feeling that he was being watched by some unseen eye. He heard a rustle in the dry leaves behind him; he turned around instantly, and thought he saw a shadow. He felt cold and alone, surrounded by the ominous and overwhelming trees. But still he kept moving, willing himself to go on.

After about another hour, he stumbled upon a clearing in the woods. seeing some strange designs laid out on the floor with twigs, he remembered he'd seen other things like this in the woods. There was definitely something odd going on here. Still, he carried on, getting the same feeling he was being watched.

The moon disappeared behind a cloud; he tripped over a root and fell flat on his face on the brown leaves. They seemed so inviting, he just wanted to fall asleep and forget everything. Slowly he closed his eyes and the darkness engulfed him.

Daniel Daly (14)
The Blandford School, Blandford Forum

Untitled

The band looked into each other's eyes, waiting until the moment felt right to walk onto the stage, into the view of the ecstatic crowd. Then it happened - each member of the band heard it. A slow chorus, chanting for them to enter the limelight. The band purposefully strode onto the stage to a mighty cheer from the sea of euphoric fans. As they picked up their instruments, two on guitar, one on bass, one on drums, the amps shed a small ripple of sound. Then there was the silent count from the band, again waiting for the moment to begin this musical experience. A slight lowering of volume of the crowd was enough for the guitarists to launch into an ear-splitting riff, backed up by a pounding drumbeat and thumping bass.

As one of the guitarists started to reel off the emotional lyrics, the rest of the band kept in time perfectly to produce a sound only praised by the ear of a man who knows his music. What followed for the next hour and a half was an epic roller coaster of anthems, sessions and classics that, by the end of it all, had the exhausted crowd gasping for more.

Finally, the band decided to end it all with one last song that would finish the night off with a bang. Once more, they waited for the perfect moment.

Jamie Chadd (14)
The Blandford School, Blandford Forum

The Day Of Daisy

The sun set, creating a drain in the sky, drinking the light from the day in a single gulp. I longed for my family to be here, but there was no way I was going back. It was clear I was not wanted at home. The night drew close, like a smothering blanket.

Fear flew down my back. I stood, mesmerised by the flames, my feet taking root in the ground. The smoke for the forest fire was thick, black and climbing its way high into the sky.

My palms were covered in droplets of cold sweat, and my eyes were full of round tears from the stinging smoke. Fear was tainting my senses, dulling and slowing my mind. The aggressive darkness was pushing in on all sides; except from the fire, where flames twirled and leapt higher than the Devil himself.

My back was to the river, where the fire couldn't fly. I had to get away, but somehow my body wouldn't move. The fear was stronger than me, and held me in its grip. Eventually I managed to turn, and start to run at the river.

My timing was wrong and my jump too small. I plunged into the icy water, my clothes pulling me to the bottom. I had no strength left to fight, and with no reason to, I let my arms fall and sank to my watery grave.

I crumpled on the riverbed, motionless, a lost rag doll, with a family that didn't care.

Helen Miller (14)
The Blandford School, Blandford Forum

The Blair Witch

As I approach the house, branches claw at me like hands trying to scratch my skin and pull it from my body. The freezing wind burns my face as the leaves crunch under my feet. The crumbling house that lays before me, looks old and unwanted. I feel like I am alone in an uninviting place. The boarded-up windows make the whole house feel unwelcoming.

As I step through the shattered door, I hear an eerie noise; a noise of someone screaming. The smell is overwhelming. It is like a rotting apple in vinegar. It is hard to keep on going, I just want to wake up from this nightmare and to be in my bed at home. I don't want to be here anymore, but I know I must go on, or my friend will be trapped forever.

I am now in the next room. It looks as if it used to be a living room, but I am not sure. The great fireplace that is no more, has water dripping down like blood from someone's finger. My heart stops. The hairs on the back of my neck rise as I once again hear the screaming. I must go on.

I start to climb the stairs to investigate further, but as I reach the first landing, I stop once more. Blood! Small hand shapes have been formed on the wall. They are so tiny, only a child could have made them.

Zoë Lamb (13)
The Blandford School, Blandford Forum

About A Girl

I'm an ordinary girl, well sort of. I live the perfect life. I'm seen a an idol to most younger girls. I mean, I'm 19, have the perfect boyfriend who I'm marrying in a fortnight. My baby boy is due in two months. I have all my family around me to support me and I'm famous worldwide for my singing.

So why aren't I happy? I mean, most girls would love to have my life, but I would love to have theirs. Don't get me wrong, I love my family, it's just … well, they don't understand me. They live my life for me. Every decision I make, everything I do or say, is what I'm told.

I mean come on, I'm only 19 and pregnant, I'll never be able to go out, have fun and enjoy myself with a child to look after. *And* I'm marrying in two weeks, talk about rushing things. Then I've got the press, who never leave me alone. There's always some reporter at the door.

I've got so much, and yet so little. I feel empty and numb all the time. I smile, but just want to scream, it's like everyone's watching me break down, but not having a care in the world. My life is so bright and colourful on the outside, but on the inside, dark and terrifying. It's just one thing after another: it's never-ending torment. I don't know what to do, say think; I'm lost and can't find my way home.

Catherine Abraham
The Blandford School, Blandford Forum

Life In Jeopardy

'I can't believe this,' yelled Mum, with tears dripping down her face. 'How long has it been going on?'

'A month, but I didn't want to tell you or Emma, I was looking out for your best interests,' replied Dad.

'Of course you were, dear, thanks a lot,' sarcastically said Mum.

It was late at night and I put a robe on and stumbled down the stairs with half open eyes. Mum was sitting, head down, staring at a blank space. Dad ran to my side, kneeling to my level. I knew what was coming. Life in our house had been terrible for the last couple of months. I didn't want to hear what was coming. I ran to my mum's side, she held me and explained, wouldn't let me go. Our life had changed.

Dad packed his stuff the next morning and left. It was so surreal and unlike him to leave us. For the next few weeks we didn't leave the house. Later, one Friday evening there was a phone call from my dad asking for me to go and stay. I was told to go, so I went that night.

She was there, standing at the door, gripping hold of his hand. The person who had put my parents' life in jeopardy. We got introduced and I stayed.

Two months on and my mum was back to normal, and I stayed every other weekend with my dad, even though it wasn't the same. But I had decided to stay with my mum as she had the stable life.

Hannah Bissett (14)
The Blandford School, Blandford Forum

Guilty!

I was only eight, not old enough to handle a newborn baby. My mum was in the bath and my dad was out.

My brother was sitting in my mum's room in a portable chair, he was cute like a teddy bear. I started playing with his little fingers, although he was watching 'RugRats'. But I wanted to play with him in my room, so I picked his chair up and then ... *Bang!* He fell out of the chair onto my mum's bedroom floor, his eyes started to fill with water, then tears started pouring out like water running from a tap.

I tried to stop him, but he wouldn't stop, then Mum heard and rushed out of the bathroom and saw him on the floor crying. She looked at me standing there nearly in tears too. I just ran to my room with guilt, I just kept asking myself questions like, was he OK? Was Mum mad?

I went straight to sleep. I didn't dare go out of my room with tears still pouring from my eyes.

The next day I was so scared to walk downstairs to see my brother. I crept slowly down the stairs to see my brother, as I walked into the kitchen, I saw my brother sitting there with a bruised face. My mum kept saying don't worry, but even so I still felt guilty. After talking to her I wanted to play with my bruised teddy bear. My newborn brother!

Hannah Manson (14)
The Blandford School, Blandford Forum

Jasmine

She lived in a small village. An only child, a happy girl with lots of friends. But then Jasmine had to move home, move families and move schools. She was going to be fostered. After her mum's illness, the family couldn't cope so Jasmine had to suffer.

The new family had seemed perfect at first, but looks can be deceiving. Mr White never spoke unless he had to and Mrs White preferred her own company. They had no children of their own as Mrs White suffered with various health complications.

Her new life seemed hard at first. At her own home she was spoilt by her parents and fussed over. At this house Jasmine was ignored and relatives never came to visit. Mrs White wasn't much of a cook and spent most of her time preening over herself.

As Jasmine lay on her unmade bed, her thoughts drifted off towards school. That is where she was happy. Family life was awkward and she didn't fit in. *Like a diamond amongst dirt,* she thought angrily.

Suddenly she had an urge for her family; she leant over her second-hand bed, and pulled out a photo. It was of her and her family. Together. That's when it hit her; she was unhappy here and wanted to get away, so why not stay with a relative? It was so simple! She walked over to her shabby computer and sat down. A small smile crept over her face.

'Now where to begin ...?'

Jodie Cooper (14)
The Blandford School, Blandford Forum

Back With The Boys

Leaving the site in a large number, the boys headed out towards the rec'. Locked and loaded with alcohol, their bags were as heavy as the night was dark. Creeping from around a corner, the bright headlights of the police car glistened and reflected off the aluminium objects and into their eyes. The lads ran around the corner, their hearts hanging in their throats, they had got away.

Beginning to really feel the alcohol's effect, Dustin was causing a disturbance. The use of his foul language echoed throughout the garden, the sound waves rebounding off the fence panels.

'Shut up Dustin, you're waking the whole town up!' called Tardiff.

'Come on then!' Drunken Dustin approached Tardiff with a stick while the others giggled. *Bang!* The stick smashed, rattling Tardiff's spine.

'Right that's bloomin' it!'

He jumped on Dustin, hitting him in the stomach and slamming him into the side of the tent. Two outstretched arms swung out and pushed Tardiff off, his arm breaking through the window of the shed behind him. All went quiet. Everyone was shocked.

Making their way to the hospital, Tardiff, Beano and Marc were cold and exhausted. Blood trickled down his arm, staining his polo shirt, his trousers and his trainers. Arriving at the hospital in the early hours of the morning, the victim's head was feeling light; he was dizzy and feeling faint.

An hour later, the arm was wrapped up, and they were back with the boys. Broken glass remained on the floor; the anger remained in his head.

Chris Taafe
The Blandford School, Blandford Forum

One Chance

It was 2-2. Five minutes left. Down to me. If I scored we would surely go through to the final. If I missed, well we wouldn't know.

I did not actually see why the penalty was given, but it was given. When the whistle blew the whole team cheered as if we had actually scored. However, there was still the small matter of putting the ball in the back of the net. Steven came up to me and said probably the worst thing he could say at that moment. 'Come on. Everybody is counting on you.'

Thanks, I thought, I didn't need any extra pressure really. Anyway I had to concentrate. We needed this after all!

There was no spot on the pitch, so there was an extra delay before I could actually take the penalty. The referee took a long time to find a spot that I could actually take it from. When he eventually did, everything went silent. It was me, the ball and the seemingly tiny goal. I waited for the whistle. When it came I took a deep breath and ran.

The next day everyone was hailing us as the best ever Blandford team. We had the chance to be the first ever Blandford team to win a final. We were over the moon, despite having to play Ashdown, a team we can never seem to beat, in the final.

And one more thing in case you were wondering, bottom left, keeper wrong way; *final!*

Alex Robbins (14)
The Blandford School, Blandford Forum

Another Man

Bright. Bright was the day that this story begins. Not so long ago in a place not so far away there was a man and no one knew his name. He was a scruffy-looking, stubble-ridden, hairy old brute. He lived alone in an old barn with only his shadow for company, he was a tall, well-built man with little character about him apart from his large beak-like nose and his weathered, old-looking face, with great large blue pools for eyes which mesmerised anyone who looked upon him. As he was alone he never shaved, so there was a great mass of hair on his face filling every nook and cranny, it fell upon him in great overpowering waves like a rough and untameable beast.

As you looked upon him you would feel great despair, malice, hate, envy, loneliness, anger and sadness. You could stare into his baby-blue eyes and be lost in a great sea forever. As he walked he stooped and waddled for hours at a time day after day, week after week, wandering the world like an unsettled soul. This poor lonely man who had nobody was found one bitter morning. This poor, poor man was found dead with no motive or no meaning to the killing. He was killed by another man who was drunk, he was killed by a man who was drink driving.

Alexander Lyes (14)
The Blandford School, Blandford Forum

The Spectre Boy

The bricks made a small earthquake as they hit the floor. Roger lifted the crowbar in his hand and used his arm to cover his mouth from the irritating dust loitering in the air. He spluttered and jolted his arm; the hook of the crowbar cut a scratch above his eyebrow. His family were observing him open the newly discovered fireplace from the safety of the dining table.

As the dust settled on the white sheet that was laid on the floor, the family smiled in approval of their beautiful marble fireplace. The smiles faded as what appeared to be a foot swung in the opening. Roger went to see the limb close up; there were veins through the skin, red, blue and pulsing. This thing was alive ...

He plucked up the courage to reach and touch the leg. As he did the leg squirmed and the creature wriggled its way down the tight chimney space until it rested in the open space in the fireplace. It was a young man. He was pale, but only because his skin was thin like tissue paper. You could see his organs machining slowly, not alive, but working slowly.

The young man had a scratch above his eyebrow, exactly the same as Roger. He swung randomly and punched Roger in the face. Roger felt pain and so did the boy. Roger's nose bled, so did the boy's - even though Roger didn't throw a punch.

The spectre would kill everyone. They'd have to kill Roger.

Raph Lee (14)
The Blandford School, Blandford Forum

Moonlight Mystery

'Bye Mum,' said Emily. Emily is 15 years old and gets scared easily. 'See you later.' She carried on and walked out.

After 2 hours of walking, she didn't know where she was. *Where am I?* she thought. It started to get dark, it was going to be a full moon that night. 'I'm lost!' She said it over and over again.

In the distance Emily could see a faint outline of a building in the moonlight. She went closer and found it was a castle that looked like it was very rundown. She went in and started to look around. 'Who's there?' she shouted as she heard footsteps behind her. As the footsteps got louder she saw a shadow on the wall. Emily got scared and started to run down a deserted corridor, as she ran, the shadow followed. She heard the shattered windows smash against the rotting frames, as if they were cheering her on for a race. She turned into an empty room, except for one old chair in the centre of the room. She pushed the chair against the door, then jumped to look out the window.

Suddenly, the chair pulled away from the door and the handle started to twist and squeak. She hid in a corner, pulling the chair in front to hide herself, from the thing. The door swung open, she heard the floorboards creak, she started screaming, the door closed and she quickly ran …

Perrie Staley-Crouch (13)
The Blandford School, Blandford Forum

A Day In The Life Of A Cow

I wake up surrounded by my other friends, we all wait for breakfast. I can hear everyone else going to breakfast so I go along as well. *Yes!* Grass my favourite food and I'm in time to claim a big area of grass to myself! It is a very dry day today so my food won't get wet around me.

After my breakfast I'm grouped with some other cows because it's *milking time!* My favourite time of the day. I gave the most milk so I get to go to the biggest field with 10 other winning cows.

I feel so happy today that I chase the other cows around and then they chase me back so that it turns into a game of 'It' and I'm the catcher! Yes!

I see most humans walking in my fields, I must follow them to make sure that they don't try and steal my food. They see me coming and hurry out of the field, I feel very offended so I give them an angry, 'Mooooooo.' I then get distracted by more grass.

We are being gathered up now, I don't want to go in so I run away from the herd and head out of the gate to the other fields where I can eat as much as I want without being disturbed by anyone. But then the farmer starts chasing me in his tractor because of my attempt to escape from him. 'Mooooo.' He gains on me, so I start running in circles then try to find my way back to the barn as I'm getting too tired.

I stop and realise that the barn is straight ahead, I run to it. When I get inside I find that there is no food left!

Yvette Lowe (15)
The Blandford School, Blandford Forum

A Day In The Life Of An Angel

The heavens opened above. We all sang and danced. We were getting ready to look down onto Earth. We all pushed and shoved our way to the mirror. I do not really know why we did as we have loads of mirrors.

Anyway, today the sun rose like a ship setting sail. The skies opened and cleared ready for us. I scrambled my way to our emergency board. There were flashing lights dotting around everywhere. What was happening? God was not in a very good mood today so I thought I had better talk to Him. It turns out that one of the devils had come up from Hell and set foot on to Earth. We all fluttered down to Earth to save what we could.

One thing that caught my eye most was a hospital. Not just any hospital either. Within the hospital there lay a man. One man who had an outstanding personality and a strong will. I touched him and told him to stay on Earth and his face lit as bright as the heavens above.

I knew he was alright, but something struck me. Things are not always what they seem. The miracle here was not from me. It was from him. Humankind meant well, but this man did well. His will was stronger than the world put together. The angels shall go back up to Heaven. My work for today is done. The Devil has gone.

Carly Morris (13)
The Blandford School, Blandford Forum

Untitled

She woke up in a sweat; the darkness of the air was filled with smoke. Was this a dream or was it real? Everyone in the car was motionless, she cried for help but the dryness of her throat left her only able to whisper. Small, dancing, orange flames came from the front of the car and the darkness turned into a thick fog. Anna paused for a minute and slowly tilted her head to Jamie, his hands were still on the wheel and his head bent forward. The flames rose higher and Anna felt the heat against her. She unbuckled herself and pushed open the door with a force, the weight of her body sent sharp pains up her legs as she limped round the side of the car.

She glared at Jamie through the cracked window; it took Anna several attempts to open the door, with the last go the door flew open as Anna stumbled back. Pulling Jamie out of the car weighed Anna's ankles down. She placed him on the floor as lightly as possible. The floor was cold and damp, she held Jamie tight, all she could think of; was it all her fault? What was going to happen now?

Anna gazed both ways at the road and there was silence. The car was totally lit as she realised that she had no way of contacting any help; should she leave Jamie? Anna knew that she would have to take a risk ...

Shauni Paulley (15)
The Blandford School, Blandford Forum

The Drop

'It's ludicrous, impossible,' I muttered to myself. My brain spinning frantically, as I perched on my bike, hovering 15 foot up, on a narrow wall. Every time I looked down, it appeared to be rising up out of the ground as if it were growing in height.

All I had to do was drop down 15 feet and land on the ground without falling off my bike. Simple in theory but the more I thought, the longer I waited and the higher the wall became. The sun crept away, my excuse to go home and try another day.

Morning came and I rode down to the wall that sat high and parallel to the old library. Soon though time had passed and yet again I failed to take that drop I longed to do. Days went by and still I had not achieved the drop. I had to do this, I needed to know that I was capable of it, it was the ultimate thrill.

This was it, the day dawned and I was ready, my muscles stiffened and adrenaline coursed through my veins. I took the drop, with one small pedal crank I was off, flying, I hit the floor with a shudder, but I hadn't fallen off, I had done it! Victory fulfilled me and the wall became just the 'old library wall', it was the drop no more.

Kieran Harvey (15)
The Blandford School, Blandford Forum

Spiders And Candyfloss

'Mmmm ... yummy.'
'Ariadne, did you just eat *all* my candyfloss?'
'Yup,' Ariadne said to me gleefully.
My friend Tor shook his head. 'Greedy as usual, I see,' he said.
'Of course.' Ariadne sat in the middle of the table, with her eight legs dangling off the edge. 'You made me that way.'
'Yeah, and what an idea that was. Making a giant, talking spider,' Tor said with disgust.
'We all love her,' Clea hugged her.
Tor grunted and looked at the theme park map. 'Oh, a vertical drop ride, let's go on that next!'
'Er ... let's not,' I said nervously.
'Don't be such a wimp, Michiru,' Tor said.
'For once, I agree with him,' Ariadne said, munching on Tor's candyfloss.

My insides were squirming as they dragged me to the ride.
'But ... I'm too young to die!' I screamed.
Clea sighed, 'You'll live.'
'I'll be sick,' I threatened.
'But you'll live.'
'No ... I'll die tragically, and you'll all be sorry.'
Tor rolled his eyes, as if trying to figure who annoyed him more, Ariadne or me. 'Just stay here then. I wouldn't want to go on with a chicken like you anyway,' he said scathingly.
How could I refuse such a challenge? I bit my tongue and followed him onto the ride, holding Ariadne. My pet spider was trying to look like a stuffed toy.
Slowly, the ride cage went to the top.
3 ...
I closed my eyes.
2 ...
I clutched Tor's hand and ignored him as he murmured, 'Gerroff.'
1 ...

Michelle Kisbee (14)
The Blandford School, Blandford Forum

A Normal Land Of Nonsense

In the land of the very warty, the inhabitants are just over forty. They live in a land, with zombie bands, twelve colours in rainbows and blue and red cows. The houses are tall, the tallest around and they do the hoovering without a sound.

The mice go woof, the monkeys go moo, the giraffes speak French and kangaroos go boo. Other animals you may not have heard of, like the three-eyed hula and the twelve-legged nerd. Cars have two wheels and wear bowler hats, buses are free and are driven by cats. This land's creatures all have weird names, are best friends with aliens and play twisted games.

The schools don't teach science, English or maths, but they teach how to burp, be rude and eat trash. Teachers are nice, they are purple and green, but their spelling is awful, the worst ever seen.

The shops have no shelves, the food's on the floor. Everything's squished and blocking the door. The cashier's just so totally rude, sitting back stuffing his face with food. He thinks we're weird having soft skin, not having spots or eating the bins. And girls wearing skirts he'd be in fits, girls usually wear banana-flavoured kits. But the worst thing is the food you see, made by giant gold bumblebees. It looks like slime, tastes like dirt, it's topped with sprinkles which make you hurt.

So now you know about this land, tell everybody you can. This isn't nonsense, it's *my* land.

Kelly Wareham (14)
The Blandford School, Blandford Forum

Untitled

Lenny Cooper is the world's biggest liar. They say a lie can grow bigger and bigger, one man paid the price.

One day, Lenny's scientist girlfriend Jenny called, asking where he'd been. So he didn't upset her, he made up the story that he'd been at Jay's, even though he hadn't. After she hung up, Jay arrived at Lenny's wondering where he'd been, they were supposed to go to a football match. Knowing Jay would understand, he said he was with Jenny, even though he was with an old friend.

After he left, Lenny felt a tingling sensation inside and began to grow at an alarming rate! Within minutes he'd demolished his house and was 75ft tall! He became this height because when he was a child a 75ft monster terrorised the town. He didn't know why it'd happened but knew it had when he'd lied to Jenny and Jay.

Not wanting to remain 75ft, he tried to put things right. However, this didn't work, he kept causing mayhem.

Later, Jenny saw him and decided to make a potion to return him to normal, but instead of curing him, it made his hair turn red when he was angry and his skin turn blue when he was upset. Lenny realised he couldn't lie any more.

Jenny departed, returning an hour later with another potion, which returned Lenny to normal. From then on, he vowed not to lie again because, as he discovered the hard way, the truth isn't overrated.

Emma Taylor (14)
The Blandford School, Blandford Forum

A Day In The Life Of …

I am waiting … waiting for the inevitable, but it never comes. Waiting all day, every day but it is never any nearer. It feels like a large hole, gradually becoming closer and closer, silently suffocating me. The fear of the unknown sparking my senses.

My face has become stiff and ugly. It seems motionless, unable to smile or frown. The deep, strong beat of my heart, provides a certainty in my life of insecurity. My hands are moving, though, constantly, showing signs of ageing. My mind is tired, but I need to keep going.

I feel as though life is passing by. People busily living their lives in front of me; muffled gossip and stifled whispers, filling the air - of which I am not part. Occasionally they spare me a glance, a meaningful glance. I know that they talk about me, afterwards, I just know it! Why does everybody keep staring at me?

My late father said I was keeping the business alive, and I should feel honoured that people could rely on me - I've never understood that. I have seen many friends and relatives come and go … life is so fickle!

Every day, the same routine, the same musty smell, smothering the fresh air. I feel trapped like a lion in a cage desperate to break free.

But, why should I have a life, I am merely a clock!

Holly McGowan Hayes (14)
The Blandford School, Blandford Forum

Short Story

She never thought it would be like this, the searing pain inside, the blindness, the shortness of breath in her chest. She was tired from all the questions running around her head from the night before. But all she could think of now was the hollow aching she felt.

It was only last week, when she was sitting in her room. The sun was shining through the window as if the world was smiling. It shouldn't have been. A knock awoke her from her daydream. Her mother entered the room. A dark look of sadness was on her face that hadn't left since.

'Darling, something's happened.'

From then on, her world had changed. Sleep was no refuge. It was full of shadows and fading memories.

In an attempt to rid everyone of their weary faces, her mother suggested they all go to the theatre before Saturday. The day everyone dreaded. No argument was made so tickets were quickly bought.

No words were said as they made the journey to the theatre and seats. All eyes were glazed, thinking of far-off things.

The colours and dancing dazzled her. She allowed her mind to forget its misery and follow the story. It was soothing.

But that day was gone. She remembered where she was, under black clouds on this black day as she thought her heart was breaking. She bent down and dropped her flowers and card.

'We danced,
We laughed,
We flew,
We grew,
It was all down to you. Love you forever
Heidi xx'.

'Bye Gran.'

Aimee Dunbar
The Blandford School, Blandford Forum

A Day In The Life Of A Hobo

'Change please, do you have any change? I need help, someone stole my sleeping bag.'

'Sorry mate, I ain't got any.'

The guy spoke as if he was worth nothing. A minute later the hobo saw the same man giving change to a British Heart Foundation helper.

'Well that's just the story of my life, no one lends me any money, they just take it away. Will anyone help me? The only thing I have now is me!'

'Hi Mister, what's the matter?'

'Hi kid, oh nothing you can help me with, you're just a kid but at least someone has noticed here.'

The kid carried on with his journey because a storm was brewing and rain had begun to trickle down. The lovely sunny day, the highlight for the hobo was now being washed away.

The hobo now talking to himself, as you do when you are going crazy on your own, said, 'It's freezing and my feet are tender and swollen. My place is taken by my only real friend Bruce, so the church it is.'

He hobbled down the street, feet dragging, clothes draping without a name. People called him 'bum', 'hobo', 'it', 'beardy', but never a nice name.

He slept, getting his much needed Zs, dreaming of what he would still have. He became nameless and homeless when someone got his bank details and took down a really nice guy, then his friends all left him. He is now just a hobo, it is one cruel world.

Jason Craig (14)
The Blandford School, Blandford Forum

Blackmail

In New York there is a Porsche parked outside the Lloyds TSB bank. There are two men being held hostage, with guns to their heads in the back of the car. The driver who is the most elegant-looking is doing most of the talking. He says in a deep husky voice, 'Get in the bank now before bullets go through your skulls. I want twenty million dollars and if you come back with a penny less, you're dead.'

Paul, the one that isn't struggling against the grip of the muscular man, says in a firm voice, 'Our wives have seen you briefly, they're clever women, they could work out who you are.'

'Well if they do work out who we are they'll suffer too,' he says with a rather evil-looking smirk on his face. He turns on the stereo and rap music explodes out. He leans over and gives his helpers two balaclavas.

Gary, who is sweating with the effort to release himself from the hold in which he is being restrained, says, 'You're expecting us to do this flipping robbery for nothing and we don't even get a bloody balaclava to disguise ourselves, whereas these stupid idiots get a fair share of the money plus some protection from identification.'

'You can either get your backsides out *now* or the shots go off!'

Suddenly half a dozen gunshots go off ...

Therese Hunt (15)
Treloar School, Alton

Lions In The Wilderness

Deep in the lonely wilderness lay a pack of lazy lions sleeping under the tallest tree in the savannah. Suddenly one of the female lions got up extremely quickly and let out the loudest roar.

At the waterhole nearby sits a green jeep, accompanied by several poachers. The reason why the female lion roared was because one of her cubs had been shot. This was it, she wanted revenge and the only way she was going to get it was to go and kill the man who'd shot her cub.

Early the next morning the other lions were desperately searching for the female lion, not knowing she had gone in murderous search of the poachers. The female lion, known as Jez, had amazingly caught sight of the jeep. The jeep stopped for the night and the poachers unpacked their huge camouflaged tents. Jez waited until the next morning.

In the morning she cautiously approached the poachers and pounced on one of the tents, not knowing that there was no one inside. The jeep was gone and the poachers had obviously left their tents behind.

Jez followed the tyre tracks to a nearby waterhole accompanied by her own family. She saw the man who'd shot her cub aiming at one of her other cubs. She picked up so much speed before she reached the jeep; she leapt up in the air and took out the man who'd shot her cub.

His days of poaching were over. She had saved her cubs.

Jamie Woods (15)
Treloar School, Alton

Tenuous Reality

The burnished bronze of the figure's armour streaked with flecks of crimson, tears in dark. Sweat trickling in a serpentine concourse down the contours of a youthful face aged but dauntingly beauteous. Brushing a drenched quill of ebony hair from her face. The woman's cream complexion accented by the gibbous shards of moonlight distorting the undergrowth and the alien form her pursuer. Writhed in shadow an extension of the movement and the nigh bloodshed it craves. Tendrils that suddenly sprawl forth, take the female, evenly proportioned warrior with curiously chilling force, belied by there from vicariously swollen form, tearing into her supple flesh sagacity.

Though the conventions of an oddly transparent dome, that obscured the sky permitting only light to mollify the gloom, even the magnificence of dawn suffocated. A lifeless limb hanging damply at the side, the other clenched in defiance to a cyclical blade. Her piercing gaze is now punctuated by a pain not present there before. She glances past the withered appendage in disgust, to the protrusion boring into her lower back, penetrating past the now tarnished, belligerent, protective covering.

The fatigue evident in the frame and expression of the combatant. Yet another figure looms from the semi luminous twilight; an inorderable famished cry upon the sterile air, holding there for an unnaturally length of time.

This time there is deference in mind and body. Pacing the energy that remains between life and oblivion, she alters her stance doggedly as the tenuous grip of reality ebbs away.

Matthew Gunning (15)
Treloar School, Alton

The Celestials

The stars twinkled brightly as the wind ruffled the grass. The air smelt sweet to the English girl. She sat huddled on the damp grass but she didn't care if her jeans got dirty. Her chestnut eyes, empty of emotion, as she stared in front of her. Her raven-black hair blowing in the wind. Her name was Maris, but her friends called her Mary.

'Hey, Mary! What are you doing?' called someone.

Maris got up and scouted the surrounding area. She sighed. It was Angelica. Angelica was a ginger-haired and emerald-eyed girl. 'Hey! Where are the others?'

'Inside. Li said something about phoning his parents. Ari's in bed. Oh, and your aunt's worried you've run away again,' replied the ginger-haired girl. 'How you keeping?'

'What does it look like?' snapped Mary. 'Sorry, I just keep going over what happened, you know.'

'Hey, it wasn't your fault. Want to talk about it?' asked the American. Mary nodded.

Mary, Angelica and the boys were in a room, talking. Ari was a Scandinavian, heavily-muscled boy. 'Mary, for the bloody millionth time, it was not your fault. Stop getting yourself down,' barked Ari.

Mary stared angrily at Ari.

'Oh, pack it in, Ari. She's in distress,' scolded Angelica.

Suddenly, a beam of white light came down from the heavens.

'What the hell?' questioned Ari.

The girls went forward. The boys soon hurried with the girls. They soon found themselves staring at an ancient city.

'You've finally come,' said an age-old voice …

Jonathan Grant-Said (16)
Treloar School, Alton

The Search For My Family

I long to set on the path to find my family, my emotions spinning, swirling in my head. As I look around the empty desert, I wish I was not alone. After days of walking, the sun is roasting me alive.

Suddenly my world turns black, although I can see a strange, airy white light. Above me I see a strange creature that I don't recognise, but seems somewhat familiar. As it swoops closer, it becomes clear that it is some relation to a bird, with huge beady eyes staring right at me.

Before I even have a moment to think, it spirals around me and sweeps me right off the ground.

I close my eyes tightly with fear, when they reopen we're soaring, up high in the sky. As I lean precariously off of its wing, I see many mountains with a covering of fluffy white snow.

In what seems less than a second we circle the Statue of Liberty. I squint to see the people; they look like tiny coloured ants.

Suddenly, I'm heading towards what looks like Africa. As we come closer, it's clear that we're landing. In doing so, a tribe of people stampede towards me.

They carry me away. My eyes start to fill with tears, as the bird flies towards the sky.

The tribe carry me for miles. We finally arrive at a hut.

After arriving, I fall asleep, shrouded by black. I wake up dressed in white, surrounded by my family.

Fay Hart (15)
Treloar School, Alton

Smile

I am a present, given when needed, at no cost, completely priceless. My life is a show of many faces; cheerful, sheepish, comforting. We converse for hours, covering many different topics, yet never uttering a single word. I tickle your face, teasing it and curving the corners of your mouth upward. Mission accomplished. There! You can see yourself properly now.

I am an invisible tissue, drying your eyes, or a laugh, peering out from your dimples, wondering whether it is safe to appear. The coast is clear. I open your mouth wide, wrestling with the sound - it doesn't want to do its job, it's feeling lethargic. Sneaking round behind it, I startle it so it will emerge. It bubbles over, causing me, the laugh, to ring out. I fill the room with joy.

I have a visible, yet at the same time *invisible* aura. Its shimmer, all the colours of the rainbow rolled into one, is blinding but somehow pleasant. My colour causes all your senses to malfunction; yet they seem to be far more acute and focused. I overwhelm you, although you embrace me wholeheartedly - you enjoy my company.

I am a dancer, freestyle of course, because I am unrestricted, or an infectious disease, although everyone wants to catch me. You and I make brilliant playmates, especially when you're looking in the mirror. I release endorphins and make you feel good about yourself. We are friends, always, whatever the weather brings.

I'm all this, yet I'm only a smile.

Jessica Parrott (13)
Treloar School, Alton

Our War

This story is about me, James Heyworth, and it is World War II. I was a soldier fighting against the Nazis, on the battlefields of France, and this is about the ordeal that I went through. I wrote this diary while on the battlefield.

19th June, 1940

Dear Diary,
    I arrived on the battlefront in France this morning at 0900 hours. I knocked the bloody Germans senseless. But I am very upset; one of those bloody Nazi pigs killed my best friend, Edward Higgins. He was shot in the head, but I thank God that he did not die in pain.

20th June, 1940

Dear Diary,
    Today I was back on the front, but the Germans were firing big rockets at us. They managed to kill 40 men on the front and one of the men controlling the tanks. My brother, Paul, is a bomber pilot. He told me that this morning at 9.30 he was sent to bomb a town called Shaffhausen on the German border. He said that the noise of the bombs exploding was unbearable. Everyone knows that the Germans have got it coming to them.

21st June, 1940

Dear Diary,
    Today on the front I was shot in the leg, then the arm. My lieutenant officer called for an ambulance boat to take me to a hospital in Southampton called 'The Victoria Hospital'. The hospital is in Netley. But on the way to the hospital I was terrified that we would have a torpedo fired at us and as a result of this I could feel and hear my heart beating heavily in my chest and, while this was happening, I was in absolute agony.
    The man in the bed next to me, in the hospital, is only 19 and he is a bomber pilot like Paul. It turns out that he knows my brother well. His name is John and he was shot down while flying towards base. He is very badly wounded. The doctor said he will never walk again. I feel so sorry for John
    The doctor has put a cast on my arm and my leg. I hope Paul is alright and he has been told that I am here.

Aidan Rennie-Jones (12)
Wildern School, Southampton

Tights In The 21st Century

Robbie Hood rode down the road of ye new London Town. He was meeting his friend Little John, who was actually excessively big; Little John was his wrestling name. His real name was Billy Boggins. Robbie was short for Roberta, which actually was a girl's name, which was why he shortened it to Robbie. Robbie washed nearly every day and had the same fashion sense as Laurence Llewellyn Bowen. He wore loud shirts saying, 'Hey, I'm a moron, come and punch me'. No, really, they actually did. Robbie's father had told him that pain only makes you stronger. What a weirdo.

Robbie got off his steed. He was meeting his friend in the local pub named 'The Fat Friar'. Little John, meanwhile, had finished his 17th pint when Robbie came in. As usual Robbie went straight up to the bar and ordered a white wine spritzer. He was eager to meet his love, barmaid Marian, who smacked him in the jaw. Robbie was actually going out with barmaid Marian and she didn't take kindly to the fact that he was having an affair with her sister, Susan, who was married to the Sheriff of Nottingham.

The sheriff came in and smashed Robbie over the head with a mug of beer. Little John started attacking the sheriff with a new wrestling move he had learnt the night before. Robbie started singing 'Robin and Little John, walking through the forest', before getting a pie to the face.

Christie Grattan (13)
Wildern School, Southampton

A Day In The Life Of A Macintosh Laptop

For the first three years of my life, people electrocuted me by pressing buttons I didn't even know I had, stuck things into my sockets, and threw me out of the windows, where I hung on to a passing albatross with my connection cables for dear life, and then plunging to the ground below, having my parts thrown everywhere. This was such an occasion.

A passing cat had started to lick me to see if I tasted nice, and I had decided to contact humans to ask them to stop this horrible treatment of what was obviously a very valuable and intelligent piece of equipment.

By the time my owner had collected me, fixed me, and looked at strange things involving badgers on my Internet connection, I had worked out what I was going to say. I activated my speakers.

'Human,' I announced. 'I was activated by the Macintosh Electronics Corporation and since that day I have thoroughly despised my pitiful excuse for an existence. I have been treated like a mere typewriter when I really deserve treatment equal to that of an astrology network. Why am I being treated like such a piece of junk?'

My owner typed in '42' and congratulated me on helping me work out an exceedingly important and difficult equation and that he owed all his future fame and fortune to me.

He then proceeded to throw me out of the window again where I expired miserably.

Jonathan Knapp (12)
Wildern School, Southampton

A Day In The Life Of A Young Girl With Treacher Collins Syndrome

I walk out of my front door ready to start a fresh day, hoping that all my fears and worries will leave me be. I have Treacher Collins Syndrome which has left me with no facial features for the rest of my life, although there is the daunting and terrifying option of surgery! People stare at me in the streets and call me filthy and revolting names, names that I didn't even know existed. I can't eat properly but can only taste things through my mouth, I have to have a special tube that goes in my belly button and enters food into my body and the food that I eat is liquid food.

Within a matter of minutes a gang of yobs are staring at me, I want to go and ask them lots of questions that will make them feel unsettled about why they are looking at me! I feel so helpless and awkward. I want to rush back inside my house and lock all the doors and windows so no one will ever find me. I feel that I look like a beast and an ugly one at that, why can't I just look normal, beautiful, like Britney Spears?

So when you see someone with Treacher Collins Syndrome in the street, don't judge them by what they look like just smile at them and make them feel happy!

Jessica Shute (12)
Woodroffe School, Lyme Regis

A Day In The Life Of A Billionaire

Knock, knock, knock.

'Come in Wilfred. Ahh yes my morning breakfast with fresh orange juice. What a delicious breakfast! Wilfred would you please be so kind as to turn on my plasma TV. It's a good job I've got all these extra channels otherwise I would not see all these wonderful movies. I think it's time I got out of bed now. Would you go and turn my sauna and jacuzzi on please Wilfred, then bring one of my Rolls Royce's round to the front please, I feel like spending a few hundred pounds on something.'

My welcoming sauna always puts me in a good mood and then cooling off in my jacuzzi.

All I need now is to turn on my self-drying machine and I'll be dry in seconds.

'I'm off now Wilfred. Whilst I'm gone I want you to give the place a good old clean, but it's up to you where you want to start. Bye now.'

That's what I like to hear, a nice quiet start of my car and because it runs on Ultimate City Diesel it doesn't pollute the air.

Perhaps I'll start in Comet and have a look around. How about a hi-fi or then again I want a home cinema system. They're both in my price range, which is more or less anything. Hey wait a minute I'm forgetting I'm rich which means I'll buy both!

£2,300, not bad at all.

I think I'll finish off by having a lobster and some champagne at a posh restaurant.

I think I'll go home and watch a film on my new home cinema system, then go to bed with my luxurious electric blanket.

Daniel Stokes (12)
Woodroffe School, Lyme Regis

A Day In The Life Of A Racehorse

I'm in my stable now all alone, it's dark and the moonlight is shining through the window, reflecting a still shadow, which is tired from the day it has just experienced.

Today was the International Horse Race and I was so nervous, I clearly remember the start of the race. My flanks were sweating blood; my heart was pounding so hard it hurt as I stood waiting for the signal to begin the race.

All the other horses around me were as uneasy as me, they knew that this race was very important to their masters. The loud horn of the starting signal hooted, we were all off, the wind whipped through my mane and the dry mud crunched beneath me. My rider was whipping me and encouraging me to go as fast as I could.

I looked straight ahead of me, the sudden urge to win ran through my veins, determination spread through me.

I was going to win this race for my master!

With one last powerful stride I took the lead straight through the finish line, everyone ran over to congratulate my rider and I, my excitement was so great I felt I was going to pop. The wreath was put over my neck while my rider held the trophy; my rider and I made a great team.

It's a day I'll never forget!

Megan Ruddick (12)
Woodroffe School, Lyme Regis

A Day In The Life Of A Seagull

I fly around the pier watching everyone eat hot dogs and burgers. *Wow!* Spillage at 6 o'clock - chips! I swoop down spreading my wings out, this is lovely except when they tell me to go away.

I walk along the pier, I turn one way, I see rich people with fancy technology. I then turn and face the other way and see people begging for money or food.

I can't bear it now, I fly trying to find food, I look around trying to see young children crying who have just dropped their ice cream. I can't see anything.

That's disgusting! My wings have just got my brother's business dropped on them.

Well, I guess I could go for a quick dip in the sea before nightfall. It's freezing - my stupid brother! I give myself a good clean and catch up with all the gossip from my best mate, Kathy!

As it gets dark the pier gets empty. I potter about a bit then I go home - which is the roof of number 62 (it's really cosy!). Well that is my day and I love my life!

Pollyanna Mowbray (12)
Woodroffe School, Lyme Regis

A Chapter In The Style Of Anthony Horowitz

It was a brilliant shot. It landed about ten feet past the pin and spun back to within a matter of inches. As Jez looked on in amazement, he realised Ernie Els had the title all but won. He could have been playing in his back garden.

The other side of the course, a man was peering through a third-storey window. In his hand was a PS1 Belgian sniper rifle. The man liked the feel of it. It fitted snugly against the butt of his shoulder. He was a private assassin. His usual fee of $700,000 would be paid into his bank account upon successful completion of the mission.

The galleries erupted as Ernie Els holed the final putt and in doing so became $2,000,000 richer. He punched the air, hugged his wife and walked off for the presentation.

The assassin moved his eye to the scope. He had no nerves. He had done this thousands of times before. There were no sweaty palms, no perspiring brow. His heart rate was exactly the same steady beat, his breathing controlled, measured. He slowly tracked the target across the green expanse. His finger gently squeezed the trigger.

Ernie Els strode across the grass towards the presentation area.

The bullet flew out of the magazine, down the chamber and into the open.

A single shot rang out.

Noah Hillyard (13)
Woodroffe School, Lyme Regis

The Last Day On Earth

Tell me, what would you do if you only had an hour left on Earth? Well, that is what's happening to me.

The grey monotone voice of the morning, radio 4 newsreader boomed out across my tiny excuse for a kitchen. I don't remember picking up much of the report but I only needed to hear one sentence.

'A comet is hurtling to Earth, we have an hour to live.'

That is certainly not what you expect to hear at 10 o'clock on a Sunday morning.

So here I am, staring at my increasingly soggy cornflakes floating in a milky sea. What am I doing just sitting here? If my family and friends were closer I'd be with them, but they're not so what is the point of dwelling on unsolvable problems?

I am all alone. Just me and my two-year-old son, sitting in silence, his nervous, innocent eyes staring at me. He doesn't have a clue, but why should he?

Only 35 minutes, 35 minutes left alive. Ollie trembles uncontrollably in my arms as I try and comfort him, actually, I am mostly trying to comfort myself.

Isn't it remarkable how children can tell what you're thinking, what you're feeling, even if they don't understand?

You do peculiar things when you're waiting, waiting for something to happen. Why do I continue to stare aimlessly at a TV guide? Why am I reading it?

'Radio 4, 9.30am till 10.30am, play for today, 'The End of the World'!

Laura Davenport (14)
Woodroffe School, Lyme Regis

A Day In The Life Of A Dog

I woke up this morning and didn't quite feel myself as I whipped out of bed realising I was late. I caught a glimpse of something long and black, within an instant I found myself chasing my tail. *My tail, I don't have a tail!*

I stumbled down the stairs (realising I have four legs) to find Mum making me breakfast, she put the plate on the table, but as I tried to get up on the chair ... I fell off ... Mum was shouting, 'No Bobby, that's Sam's food, bad boy!'

As I tried to reply ... I barked.

Mum called up the stairs, 'Sam, breakfast's ready.'

She got no reply. She ran upstairs to find Sam's empty room, uniform folded. She started to worry, she frantically looked for Sam but she was not there. Well, not that she knew.

Mum put me on a lead and ran out of the house (how degrading, a lead). After I had chased some cats, birds and rats and pulled Mum into a lake in front of her fancy man, I realised being a dog isn't that bad.

When we got home Mum rang the police reporting Sam missing and we both fell asleep in front of the fire. In the morning I was me again. Plain old Sam, in a dog bed.

Poppie Stevens (14)
Woodroffe School, Lyme Regis

A Day In The Life Of The Prime Minister

Friday 13th May - 8am

    I can hear the Minister of Sweet Prices downstairs now, I think that's the Minister of Health (or maybe Dental Care?) arguing with him. What have I done wrong now? I never wanted to be the Prime Minister you know. I wanted to be a bus driver with three kids and a loving husband. Becoming the Prime Minister it was ... just an accident really. I could have done normal things like choosing the front door colour and ... hey that's an idea! Number 10 Downing Street painted red or green! Maybe orange? *Oh!* I don't know! I make important decisions all day long and I can't even decide what colour to paint the front door! Well I suppose I'd better go sort out those animals downstairs!

    10am - 2 hours! Two whole hours just to sort out some silly row to do with sweet prices and rotting children's teeth! The Minister of Dental Care wanted the sweet prices to be raised as then children would buy less and we'd be doing them a favour, whereas the Minister of Health thought we should lower them so that children would buy more and use our dental facilities more! *How's that going to end world hunger!* Such pettiness should not trouble a whole country, we should be trying to make the world a better place! Those ministers are like hungry animals fighting over food, all trying to get a scrap of power. They want to be important, they want people to look up to them. Well, I can tell them it's not all that great! The only thing I enjoy about this job is when I get to meet real people. People who don't care about whether everyone looks up to them! These people work hard to make a life for themselves. These people are the ones I respect and look up to. These people are loved all their lives and are missed when they are dead! I doubt people will miss me when I die.

    11pm - Well, what an interesting day! After I had sorted out the argument I saw it. I saw the paper telling everyone about how I'm an alcoholic or something. Well, it's all lies. I can't believe what sort of people would do such a thing. Anyway, I'm thinking of stepping down, this life's too stressful for me. Maybe being a bus driver would be a good idea now? Or I could do whatever I want! Well thanks Diary, you've helped me realise what I really want in life, anything but this!

Jennifer Watts (12)
Woodroffe School, Lyme Regis

A Day In The Life Of An Ant

On that day, the moment I woke up, I thought it was going to be the most awful day of my life, but it ended up quite funny

I woke up and fell out of bed, my legs felt like jelly. Wait a minute, I have *six* legs! I was ten times smaller! I wobbled over to my mirror, looked at myself, I screamed but no one could hear me.

I climbed into my enormous bed as I saw the shadow of my mother, clouding over me, I was an ant.

I snuck out of my room and searched the rest of my house. I climbed onto my window ledge. I never realised how sad it was for all those dead flies there, normally I swept them into my bin then threw them out at the end of the week.

My brother's now 15, since he was 12 he has had a lock on his door. Being an ant I trundled under my brother's door. *Wowzas!*

There was a big pink book with a heart on the front. I have to steal it when I get bigger! I have to see what's in that cupboard! There was another one of those books, except this one had 'Jason & Jenny' on the front.

I trundled back into my room, *bang!* What on earth was that? I was big again! One, two legs!

'Hey Jason, who's Jenny? Ha, ha!'

Suzie Riley (14)
Woodroffe School, Lyme Regis

A Day In The Life Of A Film Star

I wake up early Monday morning and realise I have a film shoot later today. I jump and shoot of bed. My glamorous assistant Lydia is awaiting me with a freshly squeezed smoothie drink and a cup of coffee. Lydia is good, she is always here for me and she has never been off work since. I respect her very much!

After I have had my morning wake up call I have a quick shower and get dressed promptly and on time for my chauffeur to pick me up outside my crib. I get taken to my set and get ready to be filmed for my latest film. My make-up artists sit me down in my dressing room and dolls me up till I'm ready to go on set.

After I have finished my work set for the day my chauffeur takes me back to my crib, where I have a swim or a game of squash. After a busy day I go inside and relax, have some dinner and a drink. I go on up to bed and watch some telly. So there isn't really a lot to it, apart from the acting itself of course. It's just like a very ordinary life, like everyone else's.

Maisie Conlon (14)
Woodroffe School, Lyme Regis

A Tale Of The Dark And Evil Sock Monster

In the darker shadows of your bedroom, when all other lights go out watch your sock drawer for any inadequate movement, for there lurks the dark and evil 'Sock Monster'.

Every night he braves the aroma of the unwashed clothes, tossed upon the floor as he passes through to release the light hidden within the fridge.

Night after night he slips out of the drawer and scurries along the bedroom floor, holding his nose, before falling flat on his chest, beginning a combat crawl along the landing towards the slippery stairs. He then peers around, scanning the area for movement, before glancing over the brink of the first step to check for a cat.

This particular night, the cat was cowering behind the hamster's pen, so the sock monster felt he could make his first move. He jumped from the first step and slipped on the second, falling backwards into the gap between the stairs. He plummeted towards the floor below, startling the cat, forcing it to dive for cover beneath the sofa.

The sun shone through the glass windows, lighting up the room. A white sock lay slumped on the sofa curled up.

'There it is!' the boy cried, before slipping it on to match his other sock.

'How did it get there?' he asked the cat suspiciously. But the answer to that question is a secret between myself, the sock monsters and other conspirators, known by the sock monster himself.

Jack Borthwick (13)
Woodroffe School, Lyme Regis

A Life Of Crime

The New York gangsters were feared by people the world over. This group of thugs were not people to mess with. They dealt in thousands of guns, illegally, every week to groups of Chinese Triad gangs.

The five gangsters arrived back at the New York hideout having just escaped the group of armed policemen in a supermarket bust-up.

The bandits were receiving instructions for a new mission from Big Tom, the boss.

'Alright lads? Right, I've got a new assignment for you. Tonight you've got to meet 'The Black Jack' down the dockyard and get your hands on the new pistols,' yelled the gang leader across the empty hangar.

'Alright Boss!' replied the crooks in an uncertain manner.

So that night at 12 o'clock the group scuttled down to the port in search of their goal. They peered around the corner, seeking Jack's large frame. There was the boat, just a small way down the jetty. The gangsters were relieved, they sprinted towards it like a pack of hungry wolves. Suddenly shots rang out, the coppers were ready for an arrest!

The policemen charged with their bullet-proof shields held high above their heads. They crashed into the gangsters, beating them to the ground with batons and cuffing them.

The bandits weren't so lucky this time.

Jack Lamb-Wilson (13)
Woodroffe School, Lyme Regis

A Day In The Life Of A French Snail

Hi, my name's Roger. I'm a French green-shelled snail. I'm three days old which is old for a snail, we only live for about a week. We also live in fear of being eaten by the French.

I live in a field in the countryside which is full of us snails and grass with daisies and a small stone wall around the outside.

When I get up in the morning I brush my pearly shell and change my shoes and sometimes scrub my giant, raised eyeballs. Then on most days I walk vertically up the bumpy stone wall that is suffering from the effects of acid rain.

When I get to the top of the wall I start my adventure to finally make it to the small wooden gate, out of this wretched place and be free of these cows and my many snail relatives.

As I'm going I leave my trail of sticky green sludge so I can find my way home after dark.

I have been walking for many hours and my poor foot is aching, I'm running now on pure determination.

So far I have travelled 32 snail miles (32 metres), I have 12 snail miles left to go and it is 2 hours 42.5 minutes till nightfall.

2 hours 40.5 minutes later it is 2 minutes to nightfall, I have 39 snail metres to go. I will need to sprint my fastest ever to get there …

Finally I am free …
Argh! No! Crunch!

Ben Elliott (14)
Woodroffe School, Lyme Regis

A Day In The Life Of An Orphan

I don't know who I am, where I am. I am just a lonely, lost child with nowhere to live, no home, no tender loving care.

I watch children holding their mothers' hands to cross the road and wonder why I am not doing the same. I have no food, the only way I can survive is by scavenging and begging. I have no close family to relate to as most have died from famine and disease.

I sleep when and where I can, as I never know who or what is around. I find a doorway which looks pretty safe where I can sleep.

In the early morning when I wake up I go in search of some food. As I am scrabbling around in a large bin, a lady in a uniform touches my shoulder, she offers me some bread. She asks if I need help and somewhere to stay. The lady has a badge with a red cross on it. She asks me to go with her so she can help me. We get into a bus where other children sit who seem to be like me.

The kind lady sits beside me and tells me her name is Annya. She puts her arms around me and comforts me.

We arrive at a farmstead where we are given a bath, clean clothes, a meal, a toy and a bed. We then have a huge welcome from the other children. I feel happy and safe at last.

Bethany Chick (12)
Woodroffe School, Lyme Regis

A Day In The Life Of A Sick Child In Hospital

Here I am, my day beginning same as every other day. The machine opposite struggling to keep my poor friend alive. As I lay here, she's growing paler and paler, death slowly but gradually creeping upon her, waiting to pounce. I have not spoken to her in days as all she has done is lay motionless. The only thing I can do is pray for us both, as there is no one else to care for us, no one to pray that we will survive.

The longer I stay here the sicker I become. I am now just a hollow body, all hope drained from me. All memories of my family pushed out of my mind and replaced with dread, thoughts of desperation, questions now piling in each day.

As I wander to find somewhere to get a drink, the smell of fear floats through the ward. If I survive will I go from poverty, thirst, starvation, to one day the knowledge that I exist will be washed from every mind, I will be gone, all hope lost for me.

The most exciting thing for me is when the nurses bring my last inch of hope for survival, my tablets - they keep me fighting.

The nurse brings in a phone, someone wants to talk to me. It's her, my real mother, she knows that I am here, she is going to find me. I know she is. She is coming to see me, I must be still here when she comes, I have to fight ...

Emma Bowditch (12)
Woodroffe School, Lyme Regis

A Day In The Life Of A Killer Whale

What beauty it is to be a tremendous killer whale. What a burden to have a cruel name such as 'Killer'.

They act as if I am nothing to step near, like a dark, broken-down alley - a diseased alley with gunfire. They will never appreciate the true complex structure of a whale and our calming home which they are destroying.

Pumping oil like Black Death, eating, eliminating us; wiping out the unsteady race.

I fear, I fear so much to change and run. All whales are hunted, some for no reason - just to rip us away, tearing us, killing. They have no end. I feel I can never stop from this death, but to give in.

I am a killer whale.

Jonathan Moore (12)
Woodroffe School, Lyme Regis

A Day In The Life Of A Starving Person

Sometimes I think I would rather be dead. It has to be easier than this. And the way I am going, the chances are it will creep upon me slowly, relentlessly, inevitably.

My mind is consumed with thoughts of survival. How I can get from my hut to the tree to get the leaves and if I'm lucky, berries or perhaps if I can summon up the energy, an insect or two?

The emptiness looms in my craving stomach, like an unwanted guest that has taken over my existence. It dictates my thoughts, my yearnings, my dreams, my hopes, my soul's direction, my heart's desire. I do not have the luxury or the motivation to think of anything else. Hunger spreads through my languorous body, devouring everything in its path.

I try not to think of Gogo, who was freed from the devastation of this famine. She closed her eyes one night and we never saw in them the glimmer of love again. I worry about Thando, who is too young and fragile to cope with the harsh reality of our life. What is God doing? What can He be thinking about?

I try to escape the Dictator, Hunger, by sliding my mind away from it, to better days, when my belly was full and I could laugh and dance and play and sing! When I could be a child and not a fragile skeleton, waiting for death to devour my soul. I feel a total absence of hope.

Camilla Johnstone (14)
Woodroffe School, Lyme Regis

Dream On

'... And the prize goes to ...' the Queen pauses as she opens up the golden envelope ... *'Ellen Faithfull!'*

The majestic hall erupts with applause as I straighten out my white silk dress and glide up to the stage. Queen Elizabeth hands me a gold trophy, a small statue of me with a plaque at the bottom saying, *The Best Girl In The World 2005.* I curtsey to Her Majesty and take my place in front of the microphone. I gaze down at millions of people who have come to see me.

'Thank you everyone,' I say dramatically, 'for this prize. I never believed I would make it, but here I am the 'Best Girl In The World'.'

The crowds cheer again and they throw roses and tulips up to me. I catch the flowers and smile gracefully out to them.

Someone behind me taps me on the shoulder. 'Excuse me Ma'am, but there is someone waiting for you outside.' I wave one last time to my fans and then glide out of the golden-lit theatre.

The moon is up outside, a yellow ball reflecting on the shiny surface of my personal limo. The chauffeur opens the door and I step in. There is someone in there too, watching the highlights on the news. It's me, waving to my fans and then disappearing.

'Nice,' the person says.

Oh my God! It's Orlando Bloom. In my limo, talking to me.

But then again I *am* 'The Best Girl In The World'.

We begin to drive along the quiet road, but as we reach my fifteen-storey house, crowds begin to push against the car, screaming my name and yelling about autographs. I signal to the driver to keep driving ... the driver knows where I want to go. I get out of the car to see we are at the top of a hill, overlooking the black ocean. The pale moon hangs as if from an invisible thread. Orlando Bloom and I sit on the hill, staring out into the dark.

Suddenly, Orlando Bloom says something. I look at him, I can't have heard right. He says it again, louder this time. No, I am awake. Why are you telling me to wake up? What's wrong with his voice? He sounds like ... and then the whole world begins to shake. Up and down and up and down, again and again, until my head is spinning.

Orlando Bloom yells this time, *'Wake up Ellen ... '*

'Wake up Ellen!' says my brother shaking me on the shoulder.

I sit bolt upright in my bed. 'I just had the coolest dream that I was the 'Best Girl In The World' and that I was sitting on a hill with Orlando Bloom!'

My brother snorts, 'Dream on!'

Ellen Faithfull (12)
Woodroffe School, Lyme Regis

A Life In A Day

Beep, beep! I guess it's time to get up! Oh no, it's a Wednesday! I hate going to school on a Wednesday, it's the worst day of the week all because of the lessons and one other thing, getting bullied.

I go into my mum's bedroom and say that I don't feel well and that I think I didn't ought to go to school just in case I was sick or something, but oh no, my mum says I have to go to school because of my exams, so that plan didn't work!

I get into my school uniform and go and have breakfast. At about 8.30 I leave to go to school. My mum always gets me to school early because I think she likes to get me out of the house, but I don't like getting to school early as I get bullied.

When I get to school I just sit down and read and people come over and sneer, 'Oh look who's reading again.' Or 'Miss Shorty.' People say this to me all day long, all because I am small for my age and I sit alone reading, but I always think to myself, *well I can't help it, it is just the way I am.*

I am happy when it gets to lunchtime. I am always starving and my mum always packs me a lovely lunch box. Then I only have one lesson left after lunch which is English, this is about the only lesson I like on a Wednesday. Then it is home time, I rush home and do my homework. I am so delighted to be home as I then don't get people annoying me - only my big brother, but he is normally out, so I have a nice, quiet, relaxing time to do my homework. I can smell my tea now, it smells like roast chicken with hot, crispy potatoes. I then have my tea, it tastes delicious. I am so full up that I just flop in front of the TV and have a rest.

My dad comes in and watches TV, and then he gives me a leg scratch. At about 8 o'clock I snuggle into bed and read my amazing book till about 9 o'clock by which time I can't keep my eyes open. I then curl up in bed and think to myself, *why do people bully me? I can't help it if I am small, that is just the way I am.* Anyway, I have to get ready for the next day ahead, waiting for me.

Amanda Cowling (12)
Woodroffe School, Lyme Regis